If a Stranger Approaches You

If a
Stranger
Approaches
You

Stories

Laura Kasischke

Sarabande  Books
LOUISVILLE, KENTUCKY

Managing Editor
Sarabande Books, Inc.
2234 Dundee Road, Suite 200
Louisville, KY 40205

Library of Congress Cataloging-in-Publication Data

Kasischke, Laura, 1961–
  If a stranger approaches you : stories / Laura Kasischke.
    p. cm.
  Includes bibliographical references and index.
  ISBN 978-1-936747-49-8 (pbk. : alk. paper)
  1. Short stories. I. Title.
  PS3561.A6993I34 2013
  813'.54—dc23
                                        2012029742

Cover art: "Oh, happy day!" by Maggie Taylor. © Maggie Taylor, 2009.

Cover and text design by Kirkby Gann Tittle.

Manufactured in Canada.
This book is printed on acid-free paper.

Sarabande Books is a nonprofit literary organization.

This project is supported in part by an award from the National Endowment for the Arts.

The Kentucky Arts Council, the state arts agency, supports Sarabande Books with state tax dollars and federal funding from the National Endowment for the Arts.

For Antonya Nelson~
best storyteller and friend in the world

How can I explain our reaction. We all recognized Toby. But it couldn't be Toby. Still, it was!

from "The Boy Who Didn't Know He Died"
Fate Magazine, June 1966

~

*Where I awoke I stayed not;
yet where I tarried, that I can never tell thee . . .*

Wagner's Tristan

Contents

If a Stranger Approaches You

Mona

———

They'd all warned her not to snoop. Why bother to read a teen-age daughter's diary or rifle her dresser drawers since you'll have no idea what to do with the knowledge you'll gain if you gain it? Aren't you better off not knowing if there's something you don't want to know?

And, in truth, there'd been no real reason to snoop. No changes in behavior. No failing grades. No friends who seemed to be bad influences.

But Mona was a mother who needed reassurance, and Abigail was a sixteen-year-old girl. Dear Old Dad had flown the coop, out of the picture now—living out a whole new life with a whole new family in another state—and it was a different world from the one Mona had grown up in. She'd read about huffing, about cutting, about meth. And of course all that sex, oral and otherwise. If there was something she should know, Mona was Abigail's mother, and she should know it.

And so much the better if there was nothing.

That was the best case scenario, Mona thought as she opened the bottom drawer after the other three drawers, which had held nothing but the usual underwear and leggings, junk jewelry, nail polish, striped socks. She'd been a bit annoyed to find a half-eaten

Hershey's bar, unwrapped—and this after all the noise Mona had made about the ants last summer and how nothing, *nothing,* was to be eaten upstairs. But she just put it back where she'd found it, so as not to have to confess she'd found it.

The bottom drawer seemed to be just more socks and bras and panties. (How had the girl managed to accumulate so much?) Simple things. Modest. No black bras. No thongs. Mona rarely saw her daughter's underwear now that Abigail did her own laundry, folded it herself, put it away. She'd been so good about such things since Mona's hours had been upped at work and some nights she couldn't even get home until after eight o'clock.

Abigail was a good daughter, an A student, had never been in any trouble. . . .

But Mona also knew how wrong things could go when they went wrong. She'd been a teenager. She'd come dangerously close to the edge of something, herself, at that age. An older boy. Scott. That car of his. And the booze. And the pot. This had been 1977, and they were all getting stoned and drunk back then. Even the really good kids. Maybe even especially the good kids. It had been five years before Nancy Reagan's *Just Say No,* and they were all saying yes, yes, yes.

And her own parents had been oblivious. She and Scott would come home right on time on a Saturday night, looking like all-Americans. Scott would shake her father's hand, make small talk for a few minutes with her mother, and then he and Mona would head to the basement, already stoned out of their minds, and proceed to polish off the bottle of Jack Daniels Mona had in her purse, and then have sex on the vinyl couch down there in the light of some innocent TV show, sound turned way up.

Mona had gotten all A's, too. President of the choir. Active member of her church youth group. Apparently they'd never bothered to look in her dresser drawers, where they'd have found the empties, the little pot pipe whittled into a hummingbird, maybe a baggie with a few buds, the box of condoms.

It was because of this that Mona was now on her knees, sorting through the bras and panties in her daughter's bottom drawer. Now, she was really feeling around, not expecting to find anything, but also not surprised when she found it.

Later, Mona would wonder why this thing she'd felt had seemed strange to her at all. At first, it was just another silky handful of something among the other silky handfuls.

But with a lump in it.

Still, it wasn't that solid.

No larger than an acorn. Without even the weight of an acorn. How easily Mona might have passed over it, taken it for a scrunchie, or a dried rose saved from the Track & Field banquet, some Pep Club carnation, some other of the ten million floral keepsakes a girl that age will get.

It felt like that. Ribbony, or botanical, or a little bunched bit of lace.

But it was also wrapped up fussily in a square of silk, and—was Mona imagining this?—it seemed that great care had been taken to hide it. Bottom drawer, the back of it, in the corner, beneath a very precisely folded camisole.

Mona brought it out and looked first at the square of silk, which was dotted with small, irregularly shaped blotches of brown. Sprayed like a handkerchief after blowing a vaguely bloody nose.

Old blood. Something menstrual? Had Abigail left a used tampon in here for some reason?

But why?

No, this thing wasn't large enough for that. Mona held the little package in her palm—and there was something else about it, too. A prickling, a weightlessness. Slowly, and already regretting her snooping (they'd *warned* her) Mona began to unwrap it.

The thing at the center of the silk square was red, red which had dulled to brown. The size of a rosebud, she supposed, but this was not a flower. Although it was dried, this thing had never been a flower. There were no petals. It was more like—

Like a clot?

A swelling?

A little tumor?

The bulby tip of a tongue, the size of a baby's big toe, or something internal, some mass coughed up from the lungs? Some small bloody knob that had withered, almost to dust, held together with—?

With pins.

This thing in Mona's palm could not have weighed more than an ounce, but stuck into it she could see the heads of what must have been twenty, thirty, pins driven deeply in.

By then, her hand was trembling.

She took it to the window to see it better.

Jesus Christ, she thought. *What is this?*

And then a moment of hope seized Mona when she realized that it might be some small, old piece of fruit. Apricot. Strawberry. Wild plum.

No. When she held it closer to her face, in the brighter light near the window (noting that the pins were not stuck into it randomly but that, instead, they crisscrossed the lump in some kind of elaborate pattern—up, one, down, two, crossed, one down, one up, all the way around, and then a second row the same, and a third, and a fourth) she remembered what this thing reminded her of, and of the fetal pig, sophomore biology. Dissected. Chest cavity pinned back to reveal the tiny, perfect organs inside it. Jewels made of flesh. The pitiful little lungs. The stomach. And the heart.

The heart.

The severed arteries. One, two, three, four, five, and then the larger one (she turned the thing in her palm right side up)—the aorta.

Then Mona dropped it onto the floor and stepped away from it, holding a hand to her throat. *Oh my God.* And then she was on her knees again, yanking everything that was left in it out of the drawer, tossing things around her. The pink silk, the white silk, the white cotton. She shook out each pair of panties, every bra, the tank tops, and the tights, in all the drawers. The sweet little daisies on the panties, the pink roses between the bra cups, all of it scattered around her until the drawers were empty. Then she ran her hands over the bottom, and the sides, and found that there was also nothing—not even any dust, not even a crumb. Just that one half of a pitiful chocolate bar. *Such a good girl.* Such a tidy, obedient girl.

Slowly, carefully, Mona put everything back into the dresser—folding things carefully again, arranging them as her daughter had arranged them—before she tossed the rest of the room: the bedcovers, the bookshelves, the shoeboxes in the back of the closet, the coat and jacket and jean pockets, the bedside table, and under the bed—and when she was done finding just more nothing, she put all that back, too, and, holding it by a pin, feeling as if she might vomit, she tucked the thing, the mummified thing, *the tiny mummfied heart,* back up in the square of silk Abigail had wrapped it in, and she walked out the front door with it, set it down carefully on the passenger-side seat of her car, slammed the door closed, got behind the steering wheel and started it up, and pulled out of her driveway into the street.

It seemed to Mona, driving away from the house, that the streets had been emptied of everything, everyone. Just shine. There was no traffic that afternoon at all. Just green shadow. It was glorious. Autumn. Another school year begun. Another day in a chain of such days, before, and to come. In a couple of hours Abigail would be home from school, homework still to be done, hungry for peanut butter smeared on a halved apple, and Mona would be waiting for her.

But first Mona had to get rid of this thing, and she knew the very dumpster.

The one behind the supermarket.

Once, she'd thrown her ex-husband's cell phone into that one, wrapped in an athletic sock.

Another time she'd tossed his girlfriend's (now his wife's) wallet in there after having slipped it out of her purse in a coatroom after a party—back when the girlfriend was just a hunch.

Before tossing it, Mona sorted through the business cards and licenses and credit cards and laminated club-memberships—back there in the privacy that was all hers in the fleshy stench behind the supermarket—and tossed these items in with the rotten melons and moldy bagels one by one.

But this time she didn't even get out. She reached out her car window and pitched the little satin-wrapped heart into the dumpster, like a letter into a mailbox, barely even slowing down, and went home.

Later, Abigail called home on her cell phone to ask if she could study until dinnertime over at Kate's.

"No," Mona said.

Abigail chuckled at first. She must have assumed that Mona was joking. But when Mona repeated the word, Abigail said, without sounding particularly angry or surprised, "Mom, why?"

What could Mona say? She tried to sound the way she imagined an authority figure would sound—firm, unemotional, paternal— "Because I want you to come home."

When Abigail walked in the door, she looked pale to Mona. Usually she just tossed her backpack down in the hallway before kicking off her shoes, but this afternoon she kept it strapped to her back, stayed standing still on the rug in the entryway without stepping into the room, and then, looking around, said, "Mom?"

Mona kept her arms crossed over her chest to hide her trembling, and said, "I found something today. Something—"

"Mom?" Abigail said, her eyes flashing wide and panicked. "Mom. What have you done. What have you done with it?"

"It's gone, Abigail. Abigail, what was it?"

But her daughter didn't answer. Abigail's mouth was opening and closing now, and she was panting through her nose, and her whole body seemed in the grip of something that was shaking her, and then she began what sounded like a prenatal howl, hysterical but muffled, and something seemed to squirm inside her torso, and then she dropped the backpack behind her in a single shrug, and without taking her shoes off she ran for the stairs, uttering tiny desperate cries as she did, taking the steps two at a time, stumbling, but managing to go on, and Mona found herself frozen in her place, in her own horror, unable to move, as she listened to her daughter drop to her knees in the bedroom above her, and the sound of the drawer being yanked out of the dresser, thumping onto the wooden floorboards, and her daughter's terrible animal wailing and shrieking that went on and on and on.

Memorial

There was a park at the center of a small town. In it, there was a memorial to the children who had been burned and killed in the town fire a hundred years before. Their names were chiseled onto the base of a statue of an angel who was kneeling in the grass, looking weighted down by her own wings, as if those wings had fallen out of the sky, as stone, and attached themselves to an innocent woman's back.

In memory of the children who died in the Fire of 1902 was chiseled above a list of names at her feet.

The children of the town who were alive and who played in the park a hundred years later couldn't have cared less why the angel was there. They crawled on her and said *giddy-up*. They poked her blank open eyes. They bounced a rubber ball off the side of her face, and no one blamed or chastised them. The people of the town were just happy to see the kids having a good time.

But the angel. . . .

After a century of this, she grew tired. She had never even wanted to have children, let alone so many. Summers. The heat. The bugs. The rowdy picnics. The beer bottles and Starbucks cups.

Also, winters. The loneliness, the snow.

These things plagued and tested her, over which she had no control. She was a statue, doubled-over, wings that did nothing but nail her firmly to the earth attached to her back, with a list of children's names at her feet, and only three things in her power.

Stillness was one of them.

Attendance, another.

And the third power—

The fire had been intentionally started in a warehouse at the edge of the small town in 1902 by an orphan who was tortured by memories of an abusive father, who'd died—but also by the mother who'd slipped into another room and quietly closed the door when the boy was being beaten. She hanged herself in a barn after the father died.

As the boy struck the first match, he believed that it was his father he was thinking of, getting even with, but as the warehouse went up, it was his mother's face he saw in flames, as the sleeves of his jacket melted into a new skin on his arms, a flammable skin, so that when he ran from the warehouse his arms were fiery flapping things in the road—and, of course, into the wind, which blew the sparks of him and the warehouse into one house after another through that town, which was still made of wood back then.

The children were in their beds, and their parents slept soundly. Being born had come so easily to those children—water filling a cup—but death.

Well, a lucky few never stirred from their childhood dreams of animal chaos, impetuous toys, confused worlds in which puddles, stomped, would fill up with fish. Those children could continue their strange dreams forever.

But others suffered. Choked. Writhed. Called out to their mothers. Became dark screaming offerings to the screaming darkness.

Of course, adults died in the Fire of 1902, too, but they had a statue of their own in the cemetery down the road. Another angel, male, stood upright with a spear, and very few duties, and with no fear of time—which moved across the town, and the whole world slowly but relentlessly, devouring everything. That angel's burdens were nothing like the burdens of the angel in the park, who was in memory of the children.

Because, of course, who rescues a child whose mother doesn't hear its cries?

Who loves a dead child after its mother has died?

Who protects the memory of a child, or a child, without a mother?

In the blasting sun, in the dark of night, in the rain, under the moon, and as the snow is falling?

That was her third power. The old man who'd made the angel and had chiseled the names on the plaque at her feet had seen to that. Without this power, she had no others. It was the most amazing power of the three. It was the power that granted the others. The power to forget about them entirely. To love them, or not. To stand by, walk away, close a door, die.

Every day, the angel faced this third power—faced it with the dawn as the pigeons stomped across her shoulders, and as the drunks gathered up their paper bags with bottles, as the dogs came sniffing around. Every night she held her vigil, pondering this power beneath the clouds or the stars, or the vaporous brilliance of Venus, or the hard bright spear-point of Mars, as the lovers wandered through the park, and as the dead children crept out of the memories where they'd been hiding, and gathered around her in the dark.

Melody

The street lights were on in the middle of the day, and the telephone lines were humming. What was the hell was this—a power surge, a magnetic storm, some sort of cosmic overload? It was two o'clock in the afternoon, a sky clarified as gin, blanched as death, easily a hundred degrees, not a drop of moisture in the air, and the goddamned streetlights were burning, and the telephone lines were humming.

Tony Harmon had parked two blocks from the house, hoping he could walk off some of this nervous energy before he got to the front door—but the walk wasn't working. He was grinding his teeth, he realized, something the dentist had warned him not to do. He put a hand to his jaw to force himself to stop.

Except for the electric droning of telephone wires, the neighborhood was dead quiet. Even a yappy dog tied to a white birch tree in a front yard stood stone still—prim and proper, utterly silent, only its wet little eyes moving inside its white-whiskery head. Like a dog prop. A decoy dog. When he was already halfway down the block from it, Tony thought he heard it make one sharp yelp at his back, but when he turned to look, the dog was standing exactly where it had been, looking exactly the same, still watching him but not seeming capable of having made a sound. He shifted the birthday presents from one arm to the other.

This was one of the blessings of being in Nowheresville, U.S.A.—of being in a place where no one knew anyone or wanted to know anyone. There was no one to stop him, to say, "Tony! How are you doing, old boy?" He'd lived among these people for years, but they would not have known him from Adam. There were no front porches, which helped. No one would be sitting on his or her front porch wondering who was that man walking down the street with a bunch of boxes wrapped up in Barbie-doll paper. *Why, isn't that Tony Harmon walking down the street on the way to his own house; now, what do you suppose that's all about?* no one would be asking.

Here, no one had to be reminded to mind his or her own business. Your neighbors could be lying on their front lawn moaning in agony, and you'd just politely pull your curtains closed so you wouldn't offend them by noticing. It was that kind of suburb in which, every ten years or so, something horrifying might happen. A kiddie-porn ring busted up. A body wrapped in plastic left at the edge of the driveway for the garbage man. Anyone who was asked for the paper, by the police, or on the television would say, "I never noticed anything unusual. They seemed like very nice people."

Did you ever talk to them?

No.

Tony was grateful for this as he rounded the corner of Periwinkle and Martin where there was a little neighborhood park—almost always empty unless some father, like himself, was pushing his kid, like his own kid, there on a swing on a Sunday afternoon for an obligatory fifteen minutes. Or if some teenagers were slumped stupidly on the teeter-totters.

But it never filled up. Anyone in the park would move on as soon as someone else came to the park.

It was hardly even a park. A thousand pounds of sand tossed between two benches—benches with little brass plaques screwed into them, plaques which bore the names of dead people whose families had donated money for benches in their memories. Someone had scratched *FUCK* with a key or a penknife into one of the plaques. *DICK-HEAD* over the other, if his memory served him right.

But this afternoon the swings were hanging completely dead in the breezeless heat, so motionless and sober it took Tony's breath away to see them, punched him in the gut—and then he was doubled over, presents tumbling out of his arms onto the sidewalk, at his feet, sounding hollow and absurd as they hit the sidewalk.

He couldn't breathe. Jesus. He couldn't breathe.

He couldn't breathe.

But his mouth was open, he was certain of that because a string of spit rolled out of it onto the cement between his shoes (his shiny work shoes, *why the hell hadn't he worn sneakers? this was a little kids' party for chrissake and he might be expected to chase a ball in the back yard*), and tried to calm himself down.

It was okay. It was okay. It was just the goddamned park.

The swing, he hadn't seen the swing for seven weeks. Of course. It was the swing. It was okay.

And then he was breathing again, swallowing whatever fluid it was that had flooded his lungs and face. He put the crook of his elbow to his eyes and shook his head into the bleached smell of his white sleeve.

Deep inhalation. Slow exhalation. Calm down. He was just a man on the corner who'd dropped some packages. Just a few boxes. Maybe one, the one with the Prom Barbie in it, was dented on the side, but there was nothing fragile in any of these, nothing that couldn't withstand a little impact. Nothing going horribly wrong here. Nothing which, if someone had seen it, wouldn't have looked like a simple stumbling. The sidewalks were full of cracks. Maybe he'd caught the toe of a shoe in a crack and dropped the birthday present. Maybe he was an uncle visiting from out of town. Maybe he'd parked down the road from his house because he was planning to surprise the Birthday Girl (*Here I am, just back from a weekend business trip!*) Or maybe he was having trouble with his car, or was leaving enough room on the block for the other partygoers. In any case, he was just a man who'd dropped some packages and who was now bent over to pick them up.

Everything was fine. Nothing out of the ordinary here.

And, besides, what *was* ordinary?

Everything was ordinary.

Separation was certainly *ordinary*, as was divorce. Far stranger domestic situations than these were *ordinary*. Surely you could knock on any door in any suburb like the one he was walking through and find stories just like his, or much worse stories. He'd heard a joke not long ago:

An elderly couple comes into a lawyer's office. They tell him they've been married for seventy years, and they want to get a divorce. The lawyer starts the paperwork, but then looks up from his legal pad and says, "Can I ask you a question. Why, after seventy years, do you want to get a divorce now?" to which they answer, "We wanted to wait until the kids were dead."

It was funny, no doubt about it. People got married, they got divorced. They got married with all this hoopla. Miles of white satin, bad music, religious pomp, rice tossed all over the church steps. There were cans tied to the bumper of the car. Thousands of dollars worth of food and drink. A whole entourage of old pals in tuxedos and bridesmaids in lacy tents. Mounds of presents. Big, big, sacred promises sealed with hocus-pocus and a lot of waving of the hands, invocations of God and the four winds and the spirits of the ancestors—and then one day one of them just says, "Well, maybe it's time to move on."

Move on!

Shouldn't the preacher who married the couple in the first place have to fly back in on a broomstick for that, too—that *moving on?* Shouldn't there be some ritual involving a long walk over hot coals while all the guests who'd been at the wedding watched, weeping, throwing stones at your bare backs. Followed by the traditional Burning of the Gifts. Everyone would gather to watch the toaster and blender explode. Followed by the sacrificial drowning of a bridesmaid, the one who'd caught the fucking bouquet?

The marriage counselor they'd gone to for the first few weeks of the separation, the one Tony Harmon had chosen himself from the list of possibilities Melody had compiled, and now wished he hadn't (back then he'd assumed that a *man* would be on *his* side) had said to them in that imploring therapy voice, "It seems to me that the two of you have both really changed over these years, that maybe you've grown in separate directions, and—"

"So, we should just go and get a fucking divorce?" Tony had blurted out.

Immediately, he regretted it. Cursing was one of his wife's complaints about him. The therapist had inhaled and exhaled so slowly and completely that the breeze of it fluttered the pages of the notebook on his lap.

"Separation," the therapist had said. "I don't usually give this kind of, well, *specific* advice, but I've listened to both of you for three weeks now, and I think that—"

His wife was nodding (nodding, nodding, nodding) beside him. Tony could hear her earrings make a muffled rattling in her hair. She was all dressed up—pantyhose, high heels—and since she'd come straight from dropping their daughter off at school and was going straight home to read books about relationships and talk to her best friend on the phone, Tony had to assume she'd dressed up for the therapist.

Still, he wasn't jealous about that. The guy was frankly ugly—bulbous nose, shiny lips—so Tony doubted that his wife had dressed up because she had the hots for their marriage counselor. Instead, he figured, Melody was showing the whole world what a lovely piece of work she was: a woman who could have had any man she'd wanted, but who'd chosen, mistakenly, this idiot sitting next to her in a marriage counselor's office.

The pantyhose, especially. Tony wanted to turn and slug her hard in the face because of those pantyhose, but he also didn't want to give her the satisfaction. He knew she'd just jump out of her seat with a big smile on her face pointing at him, looking to the therapist, bleeding and screaming, "See! See what I mean!"

And in truth Tony had never once hit another living human being. He'd beaten up his sister's stuffed panda once after his sister was dead, but even that had felt wrong and he'd ended up sobbing into its dusty smelling fur, begging it to forgive him.

"It seems to me," the therapist had gone on, "that you've come to a crossroads—"

"Shut up," Tony had said, "*enough*," to which the therapist sat up straighter and opened his eyes wider, looking as if he'd just snapped out of a dream—a dream in which he'd been filing forms and listening to Muzak, maybe naked.

"*Tony!*" Melody said, turning on him so fast he could tell she'd been waiting to do it all along.

"Bullshit," Tony had said. "I'm not paying this asshole seventy-five dollars an hour to tell me to get a separation. I'm paying him to *fix this fucking marriage.*"

It was all he could think of to say. Really, he wasn't sure *what* he was paying the asshole for. He wasn't so stupid he really believed a marriage counselor could "fix" a marriage. Maybe marriage counselors *were* paid to tell you to separate. Maybe, for fuck's sake, that *was* the best thing to do when you came to these "crossroads." God knew that that he, Tony Harmon, didn't know.

But, desperately, Tony didn't want to do *anything*. He was completely happy with his marriage *exactly the way it was.*

Tony rounded another corner:

There was his house.

He tried to walk more slowly, look around him as he walked. La. La. La. Sky. Bush. Sidewalk. Then, stabbing light off the chrome of some bitch's bumper got him right in the eye, and although he looked away as quickly as he could, for a good ten seconds he was a blind man. When he could see again he found himself halfway down the block to his house, blinking at the black silhouettes of two women in his driveway.

Witches bent over some brew. Or suburban matrons spinning their car keys on their fingers.

Was it his imagination or did they drop their voices to hushed whispers when they saw him?

He kept walking, kept blinking, and the two silhouettes—taking on details now: fatness, thinness, lipstick—kept staring at him as if they didn't recognize him.

"Hi. I'm the birthday girl's father," he called out to them, and they laughed then, darting nervous glances at one another. The slim and attractive one seemed to look meaningfully at the one with an ass the size of her minivan's bumper. They obviously hadn't expected company, and didn't want it. Their daughters (what were their names. Kari? Keeley?) must have already gone inside.

"Howdy," Tony said as if he hadn't already greeted them, and they smiled identical frozen smiles back at him.

"Oh, hi, Tony."

He smiled with his mouth closed before making a feeble effort to smile more widely. But his face simply would not cooperate. Something was wrong with his face. Tony felt as if it had been sprayed with glue. It wasn't budging. No toothy smile for the ladies today. They exchanged glances again.

"Too hot today if you ask me!" the fat one exclaimed as if someone had asked her.

"Yes, it is," Tony said, surprised and relieved to find his lips moving. "And these damn telephone lines are humming."

They looked at him blankly, as if they had no idea what he meant.

But how could they not? That continuous flat-line of pandemonium going on over their heads—exactly what Tony imagined it might sound like in the last few seconds before the chainsaw cut straight into your skull. They didn't hear that?

Or, stranger yet, they did and it didn't bother them?

"Well, have fun!" the attractive one said. "It looked like the girls were already tearing the house up in there a few minutes ago."

"Oh, well," Tony said, and stood there expecting them to say good-bye and head for their vehicles. But they didn't, and then he realized that they were waiting for *him* to leave so they could continue their conversation or start a new one. In his driveway.

He wasn't, after all, the host of this party. It wasn't his job to see them off. He'd already paused too long. The longer he stood there looking at them, the more their smiles began to loosen—a slow fading, slackening, a melting. As if they thought he might have been expecting them to keep up this facade of friendliness all day, and they were letting him know that they had no intention of doing so.

Finally, he nodded, waved with the free fingers of his left hand, and turned, thinking smugly and reflexively, as he so often had in the last years, how glad he was not to be married to women like this—chatty Cathies, parochial suburbanites, uneducated half-wits who. . . .

But it took only a moment for the cold fact to sink in that he soon was not going to be married to the kind of woman he preferred, either—a woman like Melody—someone natural, a little sentimental, whose taste in furniture and clothing ran from Third World garage sale to Victorian floral, who wouldn't drive a minivan to save her life. ("What can they be thinking? That the world has an unlimited source of fossil fuel?") A woman without a bad word to say about anyone but him.

Well, maybe she was *too* sweet, he consoled himself. Maybe such positive thinking was its own kind of poison. Why, he wondered, hadn't he come to an understanding of this in time to tell the marriage counselor, to make a little speech of his own: His wife was *too* sweet. Too sentimental. She'd never grown up. She was exactly the college girl he'd known in Great Women Writers at their little liberal arts college in 1981. She'd dismissed Emily Dickinson, preferring Christina Rossetti. She'd loved *Pride and Prejudice*, but never finished reading *Wuthering Heights*. And Tony Harmon knew why. It was the same reason she now had a bumper sticker on her Volvo that said *Practice Random Acts of Kindness and Senseless Acts of Beauty.* "What are my other options?" he'd asked her when he saw that bumper sticker for the first time.

"Just be nice, Tony," she'd said, squeezing his arm. "Please don't start in."

But the world just wasn't like that. The world was dark and wind-swept with a lot of off-rhyme and very few jubilant endings. If Melody wanted to blame him for that, let her.

And these awful women in his driveway gossiping viciously about him—well, maybe the men who'd married them had known what they were doing. Maybe it would work out better for them. And even if Tony had managed to make this little speech about what was wrong with his wife while it still mattered, it wouldn't have mattered. The marriage counselor would have shaken his head, sighing. *You just didn't get it, still, idiot,* that soft little prick might as well have been saying out loud.

Tony walked up to his front door.

His front door—on which, he supposed, Miss Manners would advise him to knock and then to wait patiently until it was answered and he was invited in.

Who, he might have asked Miss Manners, *do you suppose is making the mortgage payments on this beast? Who,* he imagined wagging a finger close to Miss Manners's face as he went on, close enough to make her flinch, *do you think is still paying back his parents for the fucking down payment they loaned him ten years ago to buy this noble family home?*

In Tony Harmon's imagination Miss Manners had hair as hard and gray as a helmet and a completely featureless expression. His sister used to have dolls like that. Dolls without faces. All lined up on the shelf above her bed, inexplicable and horrible.

Or, that's how Tony remembered them. Which might have been a false memory. Because, why? Why would a little girl have dolls with no eyes or mouths? Had they been some kind of homemade doll—never finished, heads just stuffed socks?

Well, what did he know. It's just what he remembered. A whole row of little dolls without faces above his sister's bed, seeming to be feeling nothing, thinking nothing.

He stared at the front door, and then noticed a doorbell near his right hand. Had he even known he had a doorbell? Had he ever once rung his own doorbell, or gone to the door after the bell had rung? If he had, something had wiped his memory completely clean of this glowing button, which was like a tiny harvest moon or the orange eye of a lit cigarette.

He shifted the birthday presents into his left arm, holding one of them steady with his chin, and then inserted his finger into the eye, and the sound it made might as well have been a gunshot, so loud he could practically feel the reverberation of it moving through the rooms of his house, a burning wind kicked up by that *ding-dong,* and imagined it knocking Melody's makeup bottles off her dresser, clearing the kitchen of coffee cups and napkins, blowing the bath towels right off their racks. A cool sweat broke out on his neck, and he stepped back.

Now, Tony could hear girls shrieking on the other side of the door. Then, he saw the knob turn, slowly, counterclockwise, and then a purplish darkness cracked open between the doorjamb and the weatherstripping—which he'd nailed up there last winter (a really cold winter, the heating bills soaring so high he knew he had to do something, and this narrow strip of green felt was all he could think of to do) and which made the door so difficult to close that you really had to put some shoulder into it.

However, *opening* the door had never been a problem.

It opened.

And, behind the glass storm door (another source of conflict, because Melody had wanted screens, to which Tony had said why bother since as soon as it got warm they'd be turning on the central air-conditioning anyway) stood Melody, with one hand on her hip (her hip!) and the other still on the doorknob. She opened the door then, and stood in front of him, as if to block his entrance or to keep him from seeing something that was going on behind her, although she said, "Come in."

"You're in my way or I would," Tony said, and she gave her head a little snap that sent her earrings swinging in slow arcs between her earlobes and her shoulders. The pit and the pendulum. He couldn't help but stare. They were gold strands with little pearls at the ends.

"Can you give me a hand here?" he said, nodding toward the boxes in his arms.

He knew it had sounded accusatory by the way she narrowed her eyes and snatched a package from him, and turned her back.

But, Jesus God she was gorgeous. Even her *back* was gorgeous. Was there any thirty-eight-year-old woman on the planet who looked as good as this? She'd done it to spite him. Lost some weight. Done up her hair (that deep red, she knew it was exactly how he

liked it) and worn these tight jeans and some kind of exotic looking blouse. An armful of bracelets. Tony did not recall before in
their years together ever once seeing his wife wearing more than
one bracelet at a time—but there they were, a magnificent gath-
ering of chains and bangles slipping around from her wrist to her
elbow. She turned to see if he was following her and, it seemed to
him, to show him that her skin was flawless. Radiant. Maybe she'd
actually gone to the trouble of getting some kind of facial or make-
over to torment him.

And the neck. It was a cliché, Tony knew it, but his wife's neck
was *exactly like a fucking swan's,* and Tony knew precisely what it
would smell like if he buried his face in the corner between her ear
and her shoulder, there where the little pendulums were swinging as
she inhaled. He stepped over the threshold, and she glanced down
at the shoe.

She was, of course, thinking about the shoe.

The wrong shoe. The business shoe worn to a child's birthday
party.

To show her he could care less what she thought of his shoes, Tony
butted the door (storm door!) open the rest of the way with his elbow,
and then let it slam behind him. And then, fully inside the house,
he was hit by a blast of air so cold he thought it might knock him
right over, while his wife disappeared around the corner of their living
room so quickly he considered chasing her, tackling her in the hallway, pressing her wrist (the one without the bracelets) against the
ugly rug her mother had hooked for their anniversary years before,
while the little girls screamed and his daughter shrieked, "Daddy. No.
Daddy!"—*anything* to make her slow down, stop her from walking off
into the house as if she had somewhere to go inside it without him, as
if it didn't make the slightest bit of difference to her that he was there
(a guest, a guest in his own house!) and that, trying to find his way to
the family room, he might become hopelessly lost.

"Daddy!"

Tony Harmon's daughter tossed herself in his direction with
such force it made him stumble backward, slipping dangerously for

a moment on the ugly mother-in-law rug (an accident waiting to happen, he'd always said. the floors were too slick for a rug without a pad under it, someone was going to break his goddamned neck) before his back was to the wall.

His daughter flung her arms around his waist, kissing his belly showily, making loud pretend-kissing sounds while the other girls watched from the family room. One child in particular—a dark-haired thing with olive skin—caught and held his eye. It seemed to Tony that she wore a disapproving look on her small, triangular face.

"Honey," he said to his daughter, trying to smile, patting her hair with his palm, inching away at the same time while she continued to fake the kissing noises loudly, now in the direction of his face. Was it the light in the hallway, or was she wearing makeup? There was something strangely new and flamboyant about her eyes, batting up at him, a cartoon character.

And her hair.

There was no doubt about it now. It was getting darker. His daughter was going to be a dishwater blond like his sister. All that flaxen angel-hair of babyhood was gone. It had gone straighter, too. Not ringlets any longer. Not even, really, curls. Some kind of fineness that had frayed. Years before, when Tony had first realized that his daughter might not have golden ringlets all her life, it had occurred to him—horribly, unforgivably!—that he might stop loving her if she grew ugly, if she became a square-shouldered adolescent with bad skin and his sister's mouse-gray hair. He'd been watching her on the beach, and in his mind had projected his little girl into the future—trying to picture her as a young woman already at the edge of that vastness, tossing a tiny stone into the water, a little speck of gravity which had vanished—and suddenly he realized that the grown woman she would be did not have, could not have, the flaxen hair of his little girl.

Would he love her, then, without that, as much as he loved her with it?

Well, of course he would! He'd loved her bloody and squirming with a head shaped like a banana screaming her lungs out, jaundiced and hairless and toothless, just delivered like some kind of terrifying package sloppily addressed to him and Melody when she was born. Loved her completely. Monstrously. An annihilation of utter love. How could ever he stop?

"Daddy, daddy, daddy," she said now in her phony little-girl voice.

"Hi there, silly," he said. "Happy birthday."

"Hi, Mr. Harmon," the girl with the triangular face said, and it surprised him, his name on the lips of this tiny stranger. For one thing, almost none of his daughter's friends actually called him Mr. Anything—not even Mr. H, which had been what his friends (the most familiar ones, the ones who hung out at his house every day for years) had dared to call his father so informally. His daughter's friends had called him Tony from the start. He'd never encouraged that, feeling that children ought to at least *sound* respectful of the adults they addressed, but these girls seemed to have been born on a first-name basis with the world.

"Hello there," he said, wishing he could remember the girl's name. He knew she'd spent the night in his house more than once, and had a vague memory of his daughter lying on the floor beside this girl, the two of them propped up on pillows watching *The Wizard of Oz*, and Tony suspected that this girl's mother was one of those two women who'd been standing in his driveway when he walked up. But that was all. After that, he drew a blank.

"Time for lunch!" Melody called from the dining room, out of which the smell of something flowery and chemical drifted—something canned, sprayed around, feminine. Cake. His daughter let go of him and called for her friends to follow. An elbow, a shoulder, a sharp small skeletal something bumped into him as they hurried past and disappeared, after which Tony stood for a few minutes in the entrance to the family room and looked.

Not a thing had been changed, and not a thing was the same. The wedding photos were gone, but they'd been gone a long time. Gone since that first bad fight. What had she done with them after that night? Tossed them in the garbage? Burned them? Crushed them under the heel of her boot? Tony had never asked. He'd just come home after work that evening and noted without surprise that they were gone.

The videos had slid out of the neat tower he'd forever been struggling to build with them, and they sprawled between the TV and the bookcase, an avalanche of Pooh and Sesame Street and Kid Songs USA. Not one of those movies had his daughter actually watched, to his knowledge, in over two years, but she and her mother had refused to let him toss them out, building a firewall together around them whenever he mentioned the unnecessary mess. Shaking their heads.

The curtains that opened onto the sliding glass doors to the backyard were open, and the sun streamed in and lit up a fine scrim of dust between him and the world out there. A chewed-up cat toy lay in one corner of the couch, but Tony didn't see the cat anywhere. No surprise there. The cat had always run when she smelled him coming.

Why? he'd wanted to know. What had he ever done to the cat? Tony actually *liked* the cat. Melody was constantly letting its water dish run dry and those pebbles it ate run out, and he had always been perfectly happy to resupply the cat. Never once had he sworn at, hissed at, spoken harshly to that fucking cat. So why did it sleep at the foot of his daughter's bed, rub the ankles of his wife, and then hide under the couch when he came home? It was a false accusation that Tony had never been able to defend himself against. "Why does the cat hate me?" he'd asked Melody.

"I don't know," she'd said dismissively. "Maybe you're too noisy."

But that was Melody, not the cat. Melody still blamed him for the other cat, the one that had gotten out, and gotten lost, the first summer they lived together. It hadn't even been their cat, really. It had been the neighbor's cat, but it had preferred their apartment downstairs in the old Victorian to its owner's upstairs. The cat had never been outside, had no claws and no clue, and had never shown any interest in the great outdoors. Then one day Tony left the front door open after hauling in a chair he'd found at the side of the street, near a garbage can. A chair with wings, and wooden feet—paisley, and a bit worn, but the kind of thing he was sure Melody would love.

But what she noticed when she got home from her class that night was not the chair around which he'd rearranged their little living room, but that the door was open and the cat was gone.

"We have to search the neighborhood!" she'd said.

Back then, she wore her hair long and frizzy, and it was always hanging in two sexy ropes over her breasts.

"The cat'll come back," he'd said, trying to take her in his arms. "Cats can smell their ways home. It's not even our cat."

"I'll go down McKinley Street. You go up Liberty, and then we'll meet back here," she said, pulling away.

Tony was going to object again, but Melody was already gone.

So, he did what she told him to do, wandered for a while up Liberty, occasionally calling out the cat's name. Trixie. It was a night of fireflies and crickets. Someone was playing "Crimson and Clover" in an upstairs room of an old apartment house. Tony could smell pot in the air, and rotting fruit in a garbage can. When he met Melody back at the house, she was crying. No cat.

Had he really believed, even for a second, that the cat could *smell* its way back?

No. That was his guilt and selfishness talking—and she'd hammer that selfishness thing home over the years, that's for sure—and mostly his desire to make love to Melody on their futon instead of walking around the neighborhood and then grieving the cat all night. It was his desire to get her excited approval of his paisley chair, and his need not to look at the awful truth of it. That the cat, which had slept between them every night since they'd moved into this apartment, and which had trusted them even more than the girl upstairs with whom it had lived for a year, had slipped out into the darkness because of him, and was now lost forever.

"It wasn't even our cat, Mel," Tony said again, knowing how cold and defensive it sounded. She looked away from him. In the morning he agreed to help make posters and staple them to the telephone poles in the neighborhood. He'd gone to the drugstore for staples. He put the posters on the telephone poles, but it was useless. The world was enormous. Billions of years old. It was full of holes and caves. There were swamps, forests, oceans, not to mention all the things man-made:

Mines, wells, warehouses, malls. Hotels, motels, restaurants, amusement parks, bars.

And then there was space, which had no boundaries at all, just an expanding emptiness embracing the earth loosely and without laws.

And, if that weren't enough, there was the *mind*. Its ten million memories. Its lists and hunches. Its illusions and facts. A man could wander around in his own *mind* until he died, finding nothing. How could anyone know where it would end, that searching, or if it ever would?

The flyers blew down almost as soon as he stapled them up, and Tony didn't bother to go back, already knowing the thing Melody would never truly believe—that once you begin to look beyond the rooms of your own home for what you've lost, even the emptiness, the one last thing you could call your own, would be snatched by the world from your hands.

He continued to stare into his family room, as if he were a detective in search of some clue, when, from the dining room he heard Melody asking the girls what they wanted on their hotdogs, and the shouted answers. A grating chorus. Nonsensical. Devilish. *Ketchmustnothingup.* He closed his eyes as if that might block the sound, and when he opened them again, he saw it on the bookshelf. A new spine among the more familiar spines—*Best One-Dish Meals, The Herbal Doctor, Your Child's Health, Dictionary of Quotations, Guitar Basics, The Amicable Divorce.* . . .

The Amicable Divorce.

The Amicable.

Fucking.

Divorce.

Tony strode over to it, smirking as if it were a person he was about to get the better of, took it off the bookshelf, and walked straight to the door and out of the house with it.

Outside, the streetlights were no longer blazing, but the telephone lines were still humming, and there was no breeze at all, the leaves of the trees were motionless, hanging limply from the branches. He walked back the way he'd come, with that book tucked under his arm, following his own ridiculous shadow (longer than seven men set end to end, but emerging from his feet as if it were an organic part of him) around the block.

The cracks in the sidewalk were full of dry grass. He felt weakly victorious, marching over those. They wouldn't trip him now. If the neighbors saw him headed back to his car already, so be it. Now, he was on a mission, although he had no idea what mission it was. But he had this book. A kind of trophy. Proof that he wouldn't be anybody's dupe. A man who grabbed such a book off his own bookshelf and walked straight out of his daughter's birthday party with it was not a man to be messed with. He wished someone *would* come out of a house and ask him what the hell he was doing. He would tell that person where to go. He was *breathing* now. No spittle on the sidewalk this time around.

But most of the picture windows he passed had their curtains drawn. Only here and there, a flat blackness. Here and there, beyond that blackness, where a curtain was left open, Tony could see the back of a couch, or a doorway between what must have been the den and the kitchen offering some intriguing hint at the mystery of the people who lived there. A little promise. *We exist.* He kept walking, but there was less forward momentum in it, as if his legs had their own agenda, or were questioning his. He realized he probably would have looked, to anyone watching, like a potential peeper. In truth he'd stopped marching, was actually, now, strolling, and what he wanted to do was to stand and stare. He wanted to go up to the window, press his face to it, see whatever there was to see. Anything. Everything. At that moment Tony Harmon would have *given anything* to be able to walk into one of those houses and ask a few questions of anyone he could find. What's your life like? What are your regrets? Have you ever spanked your child? How much cash do you have in the bank? Annual income? Greatest fear? How often do you have sex with your wife? Do you feel like a failure? Are you the man (or woman) you thought you'd be?

What an incredible relief it would be to know the answers to those questions from just a handful of strangers—a handful of answers to a handful of questions put to the residents of these tidy houses.

It all looked so perfect. So made of hope and exclusion come to fruition. Only here and there, Tony spied a problem—an eavestrough that had fallen and no one had bothered to hammer back up, a mailbox stuffed full of junk no one had bothered to bring in—a hint that something was not entirely right, that something different was going on behind that front door than was going on behind the others.

But, really, you couldn't tell a thing about most people. All you could do was walk by and assume they knew something, had something, understood something you simply did not.

Maybe they didn't, of course, but you would die without ever knowing if it had been the same for them as it had been for you. This confusion, it was what you were born with and what you took with you when you left.

But as soon as Tony Harmon got to his car and saw the silver tonnage of it gleaming at the side of the street, he realized he had to go back, that he couldn't just drive away from his daughter's birthday party. That she would finish her hot dog soon, would be waiting for the cake, would be sitting at the head of the table. "Where's Daddy?" she'd say. How impossible to imagine that she might search the rooms of the house for him. That she might go into the backyard. That she might check the garage. That she might turn back to the circle of girls around her cake with tears in her eyes and proclaim to them that her father was gone.

Melody would cross her arms, mutter, "That bastard," under her breath. She'd probably never even notice that the book was gone.

She'd think she left it in the locker room at the pool. Everything would be for nothing.

He opened his trunk and tossed the book into it—*The Amicable Divorce* right beside the tire jack, which had been thudding clumsily around back there as he made left turns for days now, since he'd had the flat on the interstate, as he'd yet to tuck it under the piece of carpet where it usually stayed. What a fuck story that had been. He'd already been late, of course, and then found himself kneeling at his left rear tire while the trucks soared by him, his knees in the gravel, his face choked in clouds of diesel fumes, only nine o'clock in the morning and already so hot he'd soaked straight through his shirt before he'd even gotten the jack out from under that piece of carpet. When he'd first stepped out of his car and had seen the tire, deflated down to the rim, he'd looked up at the sky—burning and purple with impending heat—and been seized with the desire to kill something.

Anything, really, but preferably a dangerous animal, something it would have aided the world to have him kill. He would have willed one—hyena, jaguar, pit bull—if he could have, to come bounding across the barrier between the scuzzy neighborhood over there and the shoulder of the freeway where he stood: something growling and slobbering and lunging for his major arteries just so he could beat it to death with the jack, chase it into the garbage-filled ditch down there and lay that solid metal into its skull . More than one homicide had been committed with nothing less than a jack, Tony felt sure. It would make a satisfying weapon. Primitive and blunt. He could imagine it perfectly. The heft and pulp of it. The strength it would require on his part. Without him, it would just be a tire jack, but with the full force of his anger it would be stunning. He was sure he could do it, that he'd been born to do it, at that moment, although he had never killed anything other than an insect on purpose. Never gone deer hunting. Never even trapped a mouse under the kitchen sink. Never even once nudged the goddamned cat out of the way with the toe of his bare foot. There'd been small furry things that ran in front of his car, but they didn't count.

Certainly, he'd never committed a murder! He wasn't violent. Even Melody knew he wasn't violent. He'd always agreed with her and all the other women he knew that conflicts could be resolved with words. He'd *invented* nonviolence. Even when what he wanted was to beat the living shit out of some grocery store clerk or the kid who'd lived next door for a while and wouldn't turn down his fucking stereo in the middle of the night when his daughter had just been a baby and so much as a stifled sneeze in the next room could wake her up screaming. When that had gone on long enough (that stereo night after night, phone calls to the boy, to his parents, late night treks to their front door, which they never answered), Tony had finally written them a long, polite, and somewhat threatening letter, and the day after he delivered it personally to their empty mailbox, the stereo was never played loudly enough for them to hear it from next door again, and within a year the family had moved. He'd won.

"My weapon of choice," Tony Harmon had said more than once, brandishing a black felt-tipped pen.

"You're the writer!" Melody would say when she was trying to think of a way to describe someone she'd seen or something that had happened to her. "Help me out here, how would you describe. . . ?"

And Tony would always come up with the words for her, the ones she seemed to have been searching for all her life.

"Exactly!" she'd say.

When he was in college, Tony had begun to write a novel. To write, he always used the same brand and color of pen, and he bought his notebooks (black-covered) from a stationary store on campus. He filled notebook after notebook with outlines and character sketches and plans. It was an experimental novel. A narrative that moved backward in time. An old man would rise from the gurney on which he'd just died in a hospital emergency room, be taken home in the ambulance that had brought him to the hospital, have the heart attack that killed him, and then make breakfast, wake in his bed, and then dream, and then fall asleep after reading late into the night, and then have dinner. The novel would end with the old man's birth in the backseat of a taxi-cab in Paris.

Although Tony had written only paragraphs and chapter outlines, he knew exactly what the cover would look like, what the
weight of that book would feel like in the hands. He knew the tone
and sweep and sense of it, and its overall affect on the reader, and
the soundtrack that would accompany the film. When he was writing in one of his notebooks Melody was always very careful not to
interupt him. It was sacred, the novel he was going to write.

Sacred, like a cow. A *cow*. Meat, and gravity. Or, like his dead
sister in his parents' home: implicit in everything. The dust on the
windowpanes. The carpet pile. The food they consumed and the
water that fell like a hot shawl around their shoulders in the shower

Melody always told her friends and family, "Tony's working on
his novel," and then one day, many years after he'd graduated from
college, she'd given him a clipping from the *New York Times Book
Review*, something her mother, she said, had sent to her for him—a
review of a novel that went backward in time, beginning with an old
man rising from a gurney in the hospital where he has just died, and
following him backward to his birth.

"Did you tell her what my novel was about?" Tony asked Melody,
and he knew it sounded like an accusation.

"You never told me not to," Melody said. "Besides," she said,
"you haven't been working on that novel for years."

No one had even noticed he'd been gone. The party was going on
just as it had—the little girls having been transported by the force of
some frenetic birthday propellant into another helium-filled place.
One or two were twirling around in the hallway, screeching, and a
few were still at the dining room table continuing to work on their
hot dogs. It was as if no time had passed at all since he'd left with the
book and returned, and also as if he'd slipped through some crack
in the space-time continuum and come back to the party as a completely immaterial being. Not even as a fly on the wall. As the *idea*
of a fly on the wall. Melody was oblivious to him, leaning over the
shoulder of some sullen-looking little girl, cutting the girl's hotdog
in half. As she did so, Tony Harmon couldn't help but notice the

shining wealth of his wife's breasts surging inside the black sweater he was sure she'd worn for his sake. *Look, asshole, my body still turns you on, and you'll quite possibly never touch it again. . . .*

He had no idea what to do with his hands now, how to stand there, useless. No little girl was going to ask the awkward father who didn't live there anymore to spoon relish onto her bun. So, except to hulk in the doorway glancing at and away from his wife's breasts, Tony had nothing whatsoever to do.

It was impossible not to notice her breasts, not to think about how, the first time he'd touched them, he'd had to fight his way through two layers of clothes and a padded bra to do so. Melody, her back against the wall beside his bed. Her perfect dentist-daughter's teeth gleaming absurdly purple in the weird fever-glow of his blacklight.

She hadn't been his first choice. He could admit that now: At that long table in the basement of Pizza Bob's he'd noticed another girl (woman?—remember the way they'd insisted in those years, only eighteen or nineteen years old, on being referred to as *women!*)—a history major with what appeared to be a permanently world-weary expression that made her look as if she'd already figured out that everybody within her line of sight was doomed. Tony had tried to talk to that girl, but she wouldn't look him in the eyes, and then she left. Later, she turned up in more than a few of his classes, but Tony never had a personal conversation with her, although she'd stuck somehow in his mind all these years as the alternative life he might have chosen, except that it had never been a choice.

He'd gone for Melody instead, who was like a simpler, happier version of the history major. Granola girl. Bit of a hippy (although this was 1981 and hippies had utterly faded from the scene by then). That night at Pizza Bob's, as Tony had watched Melody sip what appeared to be a chocolate shake from a straw, he'd thought that she was not nearly as sexy as the other girl, and that it was too bad because she seemed to like him. He thought how the other girl's broody lips and the way she kept sweeping the same bangs out of her face over and over just for them to fall in her face again was a lot more interesting than Melody's bandana-wrapped ponytail. He thought it would be a bit of a letdown to wind up with that ponytail instead of the swooping bangs.

But, God, how he'd fallen for Melody once he had her to himself. The ponytail and the giggle and the bright incisors and the positive attitude and all. That semester he dropped a course and used the extra time to memorize half a dozen love poems to recite to her. Spent all the money he made from his job at the library on Joni Mitchell albums to play while they made love.

Couldn't get enough.

Could have dived straight into her at some soft point between her ribs, and lived there.

The first three times they'd slept together, that's all they'd done—slept. Melody, curled into his chest, his arm clasped around her stomach, her hair in his face. The smell of it—as if sleep had been made into hair. Or mincemeat. That was it. Melody's tawny brown hair smelled like his mother's mincemeat pie. Some kind of hippy shampoo, he supposed. Her neck, like milk. Melody was like milk and mincemeat struck by lightning, sprung to life in the form of a girl.

It was a warm winter, that one, and strange to wake every morning and find the sun shining in on them through his dormitory window. He was a Resident Advisor. It was free room and board, and a good deal, but it meant that he couldn't live off campus and that sometimes in the middle of the night he had to wrench himself out of bed and tell the guys on his hall to turn the fucking Led Zeppelin down or to order somebody to clean up his puke in the bathroom or to stuff a towel under the door if he was going to smoke dope in his room so they wouldn't all get busted.

In his dorm room, he and Melody slept in his twin bed with the window wide open because the radiator was right next to his pillow, and an endless stream of dry dust was sent up from the slatted, hellish box of it into their faces. But, with the window open onto that first and only humid winter they'd ever had, the moisture of hot and cool was just right. The union of institutional swelter with the off-kilter nature of that year's winter was exactly like falling in love in college. Three quarters of your life ahead of you and nothing but the moment to worry about. A botanical garden. A glass box full of jungle vines and butterlies. The climate of the heart and the mind at the same time. No one, it seemed, had ever experienced anything quite like this before.

Apparently after hotdogs there had to be games before cake. So Tony found himself following his wife and the girls into the backyard, where he stood just as stiffly as he had in the dining room until Melody turned and handed him a paper donkey's tail. "Here," she said, "I'll blindfold one of the girls and you spin her around and hand her this tail."

He held the paper tail and stared at her. Was she joking?

She was not joking.

"Me first!" his daughter screamed, grabbing at the tail, which Tony instinctively snapped out of her reach.

"No," Melody said to her. "Let one of the guests go first."

At this their daughter stamped her feet and scrunched up her features into a parody of childish rage. Tony thought of Rumplestiltskin stomping straight through the floor and tearing himself in half. Had she always been such a brat?

Tony looked away from her, afraid the expression on his face might betray the disgust he felt toward his daughter, the truly ugly face she was making, and that Melody would call him on it right then and there as he guarded the ass-tail she'd given him.

The backyard was neatly mown.

Had Melody done it herself? He had to admit that if she'd done it herself, she'd done a pretty good job. Tended, the yard looked pleasant. When he was younger he'd imagined himself with an ocean view, or a Manhattan penthouse, but in reality this little yard was not so bad. It looked green and even. He was glad she wasn't letting it go to hell without him here.

But, of course, that wouldn't be like Melody.

And was it really any better that here was this proof that the one thing he'd felt sure she'd need him for—starting the goddamned lawn mower—was another thing she did *not* need him for? He thought about all the Sundays he'd been out here shirtless, sweating, bending over their shitty lawn mower, yanking and yanking as it sputtered and died, and how, infuriatingly, Melody would sometimes come out and ask him if he needed any help.

He had *not needed any fucking help.*

And, apparently, neither had she.

Beside him, his daughter stood stiffly now, fuming, her hands in small balled fists at her sides as Melody blindfolded someone else's daughter—a girl both more delicate and polite than his own—and started to spin her around. The girl groped the air in Tony's direction for the donkey's tail, which he pressed into her hand. Then he stepped back to watch as she walked in the opposite direction of the tree, where the donkey itself was tacked up and waiting.

Like a drunk, the little girl took tentative stumbling steps while the others laughed at her, and he thought what kind of stupid and sadistic game is this. Why was the world *full* of games like this? Soccer, hockey, Jeopardy: Match your wits and strength, and fail. Publicly. He remembered a game they'd played in gym class in elementary school when he was a kid. In his memory, they'd played it every day. Scramble. A line was drawn in the middle of the gym floor—half the class on one side, half the class on the other, half a dozen basketballs tossed around randomly—and the children on one side of the line were instructed to throw the balls at the children on the other side of the line. When you were hit, you were out. You went to sit on the bench.

As a child, Tony had been strong and quick, but not the strongest and quickest. Although he was often one of the last left standing at the end of that game, it just made him an easier target for Scott Alguire or David Haviland—brutes, with unbelievable physical strength. They'd aim for Tony's head, and he'd hear the hard ball zinging toward him (like those phone lines, somehow shiny and more terrifying than a scream) before it took him out, sent him sprawling onto the waxed floor while other children cheered.

In college, when he'd told Melody about this game, about Scramble, she'd nodded knowingly. She, too, apparently, had played it in her own elementary school on the opposite side of the state from his. She said, "I just always tried to be the first one out. I'd stand right at the line and let another girl toss the ball at my shoulder and then I'd go sit on the side."

This had amazed him—the idea that someone (even a girl!) would so willfully and cannily buck the system by choosing failure over injury. Tony had longed to go backward in time and see if *he* could do it, if he could just stand there and be eliminated by a soft toss rather than fighting it out until the inevitable and painful end. And what would it mean to him if he could have? If they'd yelled *Sissy* at him, could he have stood it? Or would they not have yelled *Sissy*? Would his classmates, perhaps, have seen it as the bold move of a very brave boy, a boy much smarter and more capable than they had ever even imagined being? Might his boldness, perhaps, have brought the whole charade of Scramble to a screeching halt? Would the gym teacher have found something genuinely amusing for them to play instead? Something that didn't require pain, and losers?

But of course Tony could never have done it. Tony was nothing like Melody. And, back in those early days of their relationship, that had been the whole point of such pillow talk, to discover over and over again how alien a creature she was. A better, smarter creature. A creature completely lacking in irony and anger and malice, and better off for it. On the surface, they had things in common. Their English majors, for instance. But Melody was the kind of English major completely devoted to reading books and talking about them, with no ulterior motives and no future plans—as if there would be some kind of future in that, as if you could get a license and go off into the world explaining your feelings about books to other people and get paid for it. And she was a genius at it. Her analyses of books were often more interesting than the books themselves, even if she only liked the ones with happy endings.

Tony was, however, an English major because he'd claimed nothing else and time was running out and he was a junior who'd taken nothing but literature courses for no real reason other than that they met, often, in the evenings or late afternoons, and he liked to sleep in.

Also, he had a knack for faking his way through lit classes with all A's, intuiting early on that ninety percent of one's success or failure in a literature course (not to mention the mood of the instructor) depended on whether or not the student participated in class discussion:

"In 'The Yellow Wallpaper,' does the wife have a choice other than to go mad?"

Tony really had no answer for that, so he would, instead, be the student who asked the question. It was a way of participating, generating participation—avoiding and initiating controversial discussions at the same time. The professor, or lecturer, or teaching assistant (it didn't matter which one, they were all equally touched and grateful and singled him out as an English major and an A student right away) would heave a sigh of relief and lean back in his or her chair. The other students seemed to admire him, and only that woman (girl?) with the black hair—the history major from the basement of Pizza Bob's—seemed ever to notice what he was up to.

Like him, she seemed to have wandered into more than her share of literature classes with just as little interest in literature, and when he asked his questions, she always made a funny little pursing kiss with her lips and looked at him longer than was necessary.

Well, maybe he couldn't fool her, but Tony could fake it for the instructors, so homework never interfered with his relationship with Melody. Neither did work. She would come to the library where he worked part-time while he stamped books, sometimes sitting on his lap.

He'd had, by this time, a few girlfriends, but Melody was the first one with whom he'd slept in the same bed night after night after night. He learned how to slip out of bed to go to the john without waking her up. He learned how to match his breathing to another person's as sleep came on. And from Melody he learned about biology—the female side of things. Together they paged through a borrowed copy of *Our Bodies, Our Selves*, looking for a better method of contraception than the one they were using, which was coitus interruptus. With her, he studied the line-illustration of the internal organs of the female with care. The cervix seemed particularly mysterious, being neither flesh, actually, nor an organ. A sea animal sort of thing. There was nothing in the male anatomy to compare it to, as far as he could tell. Tony read about the incredible sensitivity of the clitoris, and felt jealous. He read of the many diseases of the female reproductive organs, and felt relieved. He studied the symptoms of the diseases—mostly pain and itching—and the way men passed on the diseases, as lovers, and then ignored them as doctors and actively encouraged them as politicians and oppressors. He was aghast when he saw the photographs of naked pregnant women, although he pretended not to be.

"Isn't that beautiful?" Melody had said.

"Hell, yes," he agreed.

But something blocked his throat—mucus, phlegm?—and Melody seemed to notice.

"Don't you think that's beautiful?" she asked again.

"Yeah," he said, "Definitely. Yes." But she looked at him longer than she usually did.

Soon after that, Melody stopped shaving her armpits or her legs. "Do you mind?" she asked, holding up her arm, under which a little nest had grown. "It's just so unnatural, shaving."

No. It didn't matter to him in the least. He liked it. The muskier she was the more she seemed like another human being—not like his other girlfriends who smelled like Pine Sol and looked like pictures. They had sex straight through her periods. Cunnilingus even! Blood on everything. Yes! On his face, in his hair, on the dormitory walls. They had sex straight through the winter until it was spring, and the lawn of the college commons was hopping around with pregnant birds. On his way to class one morning, Tony crushed a pale blue egg under his shoe by accident, and gagged, scraping it off with a leaf. *Everything* was having sex.

This was, of course, the common life, but *his* common life was animated by an extraordinary love. No one had ever loved this way before. Technicolor! Tony was charmed! He'd been chosen! This was your Average Joe pumped full of light and oxygen and set afloat.

After the semester ended, Tony and Melody moved out of the dorm into a sublet together. He would walk down the street on his way to his job at the library, and suddenly be transported by the realization that, back at the studio apartment, his girlfriend was rinsing out his cereal bowl! It was incredible, waking every morning next to Melody, or waking to hear her puttering around in their kitchen (only a few feet from their bed on the other side of a plywood partition) making a pot of coffee for them. It was incredible, finding her beaded earrings on the bathroom sink. Her toothbrush leaning casually next to his in the toothbrush holder! It was only for the month of May and half of June, but in that span of time they became an elderly couple, complete with routine and cat (until it got out.) Simple chores became an adventure in adulthood, in manhood. Tying up the garbage bag to take it to the trash can. ("Sweetheart, I'm taking out the garbage now!" "Okay, hon. Thanks!") It was as if, when he did these chores, he became his own father, and also an entirely new man. The first man. When Tony found Melody at the kitchen sink rinsing out their coffee cups, he felt such a rush of pleasure and satisfaction he had to wonder if this was normal. Had his father felt this way watching his mother fold the laundry? Had any man *ever* felt this way?

But he'd also known what was coming. After their nearly two months of bliss, their two-month separation. Still, he hadn't known that he would be sick with anxiety (literally sick—feverish, nauseated) when Melody went off to Camp Wishy-Washy to be a summer counselor. ("Tony, don't make fun of it!")

A moat of time. A penal institution of time. Threatening everything. Undermining every crystalline detail of his ecstatic existence.

It would be the end of this perfect world, he knew. And he'd been right. They were still together after those two months were over, but nothing was ever the same.

The second girl pinned her donkey's tail exactly at the spot where the poster-donkey lacked a tail. Obviously, she'd been peeking out from beneath her blindfold, but this girl was a born actress, had even pretended to walk completely in the wrong direction for six or seven paces, pretended to grope the air in the right direction, before, bingo!, she pinned the tail on the donkey.

Tony's daughter wasn't fooled, either, and shouted, "You were peeking!"

"No I wasn't!" the other girl snapped back with what sounded like practiced defensiveness—a girl with a sister, probably older, was Tony's guess, and his daughter seemed to sense this girl's superiority when it came to such arguments, and dropped it.

"Next girl!" Melody chimed in. She was expert, as always, at keeping things moving. No matter what it was, Melody knew that if you rushed at it fast enough with a broom in your hand you could sweep it under the carpet before anyone noticed it was there.

Melody hadn't been gone to Camp Wishy-Washy for two nights before Tony had started flipping out. Drank a lot of beer in front of the fuzzy black-and-white TV before he fell asleep, and then woke up in their sublet bed in the morning feeling as if he'd been punched hard right between his ribs.

"I miss you," he said to her picture, held by a black magnet to the fridge.

"I miss you," he said, leaning into his own reflection at the bathroom mirror, letting the pathos breathe its steam all over his face, smelling like beer.

But it was a lot worse than missing her. It was like grief. She was dead. He called in sick to his job at the library, and started drinking beer right after he finished his bowl of Grape Nuts in the morning. He lay on their bed. The ceiling was a swirling mess of plaster and paint, and beyond it were layers of shit he couldn't even imagine. Insulation. Wires. Sawdust. When he closed his eyes he didn't see Melody. He saw, instead, what he could only have described as an artist's rendering of a guy named Bud.

Bud was the lifeguard Melody had slept with at Camp Wishy-Washy the year before. She hadn't described Bud to him, so Tony Harmon had created a picture of Bud from the tics and features of guys he'd felt intimidated by in the past.

Bud had the piercing blue eyes of his sister's last boyfriend, the one who'd called him Squirtlet. He had the shaggy blond hair of a guy he'd gone to high school with, a guy who'd played electric guitar in a band, who Tony always suspected his own girlfriend, Cindy Malofsky, had a crush on (although she denied it tearfully in his car and in the cafeteria and once on her knees at a playground while the mother of some toddler playing in the sand eyed them suspiciously). Tony couldn't have told you where the mouth of Bud came from. Mark Spitz, maybe. Some godlike swimmer. The chipped front tooth of a frat boy who'd come to Behavior Modification every day, snow or shine, wearing a muscle shirt while the girls practically fell out of their desks to get a better look at his rippling and hairless flesh.

The pain of looking into Bud's face was terrible—like seeing his own inadequacies under a microscope—but it was all Tony could do. Look. That artist's rendering was tattooed on his eyelids. It didn't matter how much beer he drank, it was still there.

And Melody's first phone call from camp to him (from some cabin office, shouting over the background noise of a lot of rowdy teenagers) made things worse. He pictured her in her short-shorts, wearing love-beads and braids, with Bud standing in the doorway behind her feeling her up with his eyes. It didn't matter that she'd sworn up and down that Bud wasn't going to be there this summer, that Bud had gone up to Alaska this year to fish on the big boats (whatever the hell the "big boats" meant: Melody always said it as if it were common knowledge that the waters of Alaska were full of large and small boats, and we all knew which kind of boat Bud would be on) and, besides, she had no feelings for Bud anymore. "I'm with *you*."

Tony shouted into the phone, hoping it was loud enough for Bud in the background to hear, "I love you!" and she whispered it hoarsely back. "I love you, too."

It had lasted only four minutes, that call, but Tony lay with the phone in his hand for hours afterward, drunk on his back on their bed, playing it over and over in his mind.

Was it his imagination, or had she emphasized the word *too?*

"I love you, *too.*"

("'I love you, *too,*' the beautiful girl whispered, impatiently . . ." was the way he'd write it in a story.)

And when could she call him again, he'd demanded to know. *Please, Melody, when will you call again so I can be sure to be home?*

But she just couldn't be sure. Day after tomorrow if they had some free time to get up to the cabin where the only phone at Camp Wishy-Washy was. "They really discourage phone calls here," she'd said. She might as well have said they were urging her to put a gun in his mouth and pull the trigger. "I have to go," she'd said. "I'm so sorry. . . . Like ten people are waiting for this phone."

Tony had said nothing. She kept saying good-bye apologetically until he'd forced her to hang up to his nothing. Then, for a long time he'd kept the phone to his ear as he listened to the dead air, almost hoping he'd hear something he could hold against her— maybe a click, and then the line to Wishy-Washy reconnected: "Hello? Hello? This is Bud, Bud the lifeguard. Who's still hanging on to this connection?"

But the connection just hummed itself into dial-tone eventually, and then a recording came on politely asking him to hang up and try his call again, and then that turned into a high pitched screeching that was supposed to scare him into slamming down the receiver— but he still didn't. He threw up, drank some coffee, went back to bed, where he stayed, and then in the middle of the night he got in his car and drove straight up to Camp Wishy-Washy—probably driving a hundred miles and hour, but he didn't remember anything about the drive except stopping at a filling station. There was a hole in his gas tank, so Tony could only put a few gallons in it at a time, and when the gas started splashing onto the black-top, the kid who was pumping it said, "Hey, there's a hole in your gas tank."

"I don't have a gas tank," Tony said flatly, and the kid just stared at him.

A sign nailed to a post marking a rutted dirt road said, WELCOME TO CAMP MICHI-WAU-LU-K.

"Fuck you," Tony said to it, and stopped, looking ahead. He knew his old Honda would never make it down that road. The car only weighed about twenty pounds and the tires were smooth as glass, so Tony parked it under the sign and started to walk. This was really the woods. There were things flying and whining in his ears. He was that prince cutting his way through the vines to get at Sleeping Beauty. He walked for miles without hearing anything but those insects and the wind flapping around in the leaves.

The cheater won the prize. A little goody-bag. The only thing Tony Harmon knew for sure was in that goody-bag was a whistle, because the cheater started running in circles blowing it so loudly he finally had to put his fingers in his ears.

"Cake!" Melody shouted loudly enough to be heard over it all as she stepped off the deck into the backyard bearing it, in flames. She placed the cake in front of their daughter, and Tony had to hold himself back from blowing out the candles, which seemed like an absurdly dangerous thing to put in front of a little girl with long hair. But his daughter blew them out faster than he could have, and then screamed, over and over again in triumph, clearly trying to over-shadow the game winner with her whistle.

The cake itself was like some sort of surrealist representation of a vagina—all pink at the center surrounded by pinker roses made of frosting but looking a lot like damp flesh, and a miniature Barbie doll doing a go-go dance in a bathing suit at the center. "Can you please go in and get the soda and the ice bucket?" Melody asked him wearily as he stared at it.

"Of course," Tony said, and turned toward the house. There was certainly no reason for her to have said it as though she expected him to refuse, or to explode. He was only too happy to go inside and get whatever she wanted him to get.

Stepping through the sliding glass doors, the cold of the air-conditioned interior came again as a shock. He hadn't realized, until it began to evaporate on his skin in the kitchen, that he was drenched in sweat. Tony stood in the kitchen and looked around until he located three big plastic bottles of soda waiting for him on the counter, and the ice bucket, which was also sweating and had left a ring of water on the kitchen table.

Jesus.

That would take the finish right off the cherry, and Melody would probably blame him, but Tony couldn't have cared less. There was no way he was going to wipe off that ring. Fuck the ring. Fuck the table. He grabbed the three warm bottles in one arm and the ice bucket in the other, and stomped through the kitchen. He was about to put everything down again to free himself up to open the glass doors when he thought about the water working away on the finish of the table:

No, it wasn't his table anymore, but his daughter was going to be sitting at that table for the next ten years, he supposed. That little blotchy baby covered with blood and goop squirming under a heat-lamp would soon be a sullen teenager eating a lettuce leaf and a scoop of cottage cheese for dinner some night at that table, and she'd look at the water ring on what might once have been the family's lovely kitchen table (her father and mother had bought it together at Handcrafters the year they'd moved into the house on Periwinkle Lane) and see how stained and shabby and ugly it had become in only a decade, and she'd think, *God, I hate this life.* Tony vividly remembered thinking similar things about his own life when he was a kid while looking at the plaid couch in the living room or his mother's ratty slippers on the bathroom rug. So, he put the soda bottles and ice bucket down and went back inside, grabbed the rag Melody always kept tucked into the handle of the refrigerator door ("Don't wipe your *hands* on that; it's just for the counters"), and wiped the ring.

There.

He felt good about it.

He'd spared them something.

He was tucking the towel back into its spot, and then Melody was tapping on the sliding glass doors. "We, need, soda," she said, mouthing on the other side exaggeratedly in case he couldn't hear her through the window, although he could hear her perfectly, and then she cocked her head in that crazy-robin way she had that made him want to kill, and mouthed, "What, are, you, doing?"

"What are you doing here?" Melody asked. It was early evening by the time he got down to the cabins. It had only taken an hour or so for him to walk the rutted dirt road to the Welcome Cabin, but by then the sun was in the middle of the sky bearing down in green-gold beams of light that crisscrossed each other in the clearing, where an old school bus was parked and empty. (He'd even stepped inside, to make sure it was empty.) There'd been no one in the Welcome Cabin to welcome him or to tell him where he might find his girl-friend who was a counselor at this camp, so Tony had started walk-ing down a footpath he'd chosen from three other possible foot-paths, and had walked down it for a long time until it dead-ended at a very small dark lake on which a few rowboats knocked against a weedy dock lazily in the light breeze, and he stopped.

There had been a humming overhead—cicadas, but not like the ones he usually heard in jagged bursts in the summers where he grew up. Here, there were hundreds and thousands of cicadas hum-ming invisibly overhead, making a somehow shiny and impenetra-ble music, the kind of music an orchestra full of mirrors might have made.

Tony stood at the edge of that lake and watched the random knock-knockings of the rowboats for a while, and then went to the edge, and pissed into it—a bright golden arch which hit the surface of that darkness and smashed it into jigsaw pieces.

Tony opened the door and handed the ice bucket to Melody and carried the soda bottles, their necks dangling between the fingers of one hand, out into heat. At the picnic table his daughter was doing what looked like some kind of Irish jig on the picnic table bench. She had pink icing all over her mouth.

"I'm here to see you," he'd said.

Melody was wearing the cutoffs he loved more than everything else in the world put together. There was a frayed rip right under the left cheek of her ass, which gave a glimpse of the white flesh there and made his heart race every time he noticed it again. There were seven or eight depressed-looking teenage girls around her—every one of them butt-ugly—and Melody, at the center, like a lily in a field of thistles.

"Oh," she said. She started shaking her head. "Oh my God."

"I need to talk to you," Tony said later, back in the kitchen, after Melody had cleared the mess off the picnic table and left the girls to run in insane circles in the backyard neighing like horses. Her back was to him as she leaned over the garbage can, hauled out from under the kitchen sink. She was scraping frosting off a fork with a knife. It was one of those hopeless activities, one of the millions of Sisyphean tasks Tony had watched his wife perform in the years since she'd become a mother. Pointless, endless tasks. She always had a bottomless list of chores that would only get done in order to need to be done again. Feed the baby, wash the clothes, water the plants, wipe the counters, load the dishwasher.

Surely it was this life of mindless detail that had turned her against him—not anything he'd done, not a lack of love. She just didn't know it. She was such a good woman, the kind of woman who would want to believe she loved her own virtues, who enjoyed her duties.

But who could love these duties? For God's sake, Tony had learned *that* much about women in college. That they hated housework and blamed men for it. He'd read *The Women's Room.* He'd read *The Awakening.* Melody, who'd quit reading as soon as she was out of college, had understood herself less than he understood her. *The Feminine Mystique. Herland.* He knew what she wanted, what she *needed.*

"I need to talk to you."

She said nothing.

"Look," Tony said, touching her arm lightly. She didn't pull away, but she didn't stop what she was doing either.

Outside, he could hear the neighing turn to screaming—some kind of whining followed by a shout, and then what sounded like a chant, a few girls chanting a nursery rhyme in a chorus. Through the window over the kitchen sink he could only see the sun on their hair. Shining and whipped about, the flash of a rope, light bouncing off something rubbery and white that must have been the sole of a little girl's shoe tossed into the air.

And *children!*

What fools they'd been to think that they should have one, and in this way! That their child would blossom and bring them joy if they raised her in this place. Mall rats and sitcom watchers. They should have moved to Greece, had a baby there, lived near the sea. Or bought a little farm. Home-schooled her. *Shoot Your Television* was a bumper sticker Tony actually loved. He should have shot their television. If he bought a gun, he still could.

"I don't think this is a good time to talk," Melody said.

"When would be a good time to talk?" Tony asked.

When he'd called a few weeks ago and told her he needed to talk to her she said she didn't want to talk on the phone. He'd hung up and immediately gone to the west corner of his apartment living room and ripped a large strip of the wall-to-wall carpeting up. Under that carpet, there were just ugly plywood boards, sawdust, loose tacks.

"When would be a good time to talk?" he repeated.

"I don't know," Melody said. She threw the silverware she'd been scraping into the little basket in the dishwasher and stood up, facing him.

Jesus. She was a hundred times more beautiful than she'd been when she was younger. Back then, he'd have had to admit, there was something a bit blank, slightly asexual, about her face. Unformed, unopinionated, a fresh slate. He could still see her sipping that chocolate shake or whatever she'd had in that lidded paper cup at Pizza Bob's, that sweet-seeming thing she was sucking up when he'd met her, and the first glimpse he'd had of her childhood bedroom when she'd brought him home to meet her parents. That narrow white shelf on the wall lined with paperbacks—Go Ask Alice, Love Story, Jaws, The Bell Jar, Jonathan Livingston Seagull. And a banner tacked to the flowered wallpaper. THE CLASS OF SEVENTY-NINE.

Tony had known instantly that, had they gone to the same high school, he would have despised her, that she was precisely the kind of girl he would have despised. He'd been editor of the newspaper, constantly on the verge of being expelled for something he'd published or written. He'd played drums in a jazz band. Hated music you could hear on the radio. The girls he'd liked had smoked cigarettes and written angry poetry, listened to Patti Smith. It's why he'd been attracted to that other girl, the history major with her sleepy eyes, radiating dissatisfaction. *She* could have been a novelist's wife. Either that or she'd have knocked the stupid notion of writing a novel out of his head in one biting remark, and he could have gotten on with his life.

But somehow, and wonderfully, over the years, Melody had *become* that history major. Now, sure, there were lines around her eyes, some kind of tugging going on there, and she looked her age, but she also looked like a woman who knew things about the world, things she'd rather not divulge, but could divulge, if push came to shove. There was something, too, he supposed, about *mothers*. All that potential ferocity. *Touch my baby, and I'll rip your throat out.*

And her body. Completely familiar, every curve and freckle, the smell and the taste of it. He could have made his way blindfolded through a stadium full of naked women and found his way to her. She had been one part of what he'd wanted, back then, and now she'd become the other part as well. It was incredible, really. He put his hand on the side of her face, and it surprised him that she didn't flinch away. "Please," was all she said, shaking her head, sending those dangling pearls swinging in their slow arcs.

"Please what?" Tony asked.

"Please don't make this so much harder than it has to be."

"I just need to say a couple of things, that's all," he said.

"Parents are going to start pulling in here to get their girls," Melody said. "This isn't a good time to say them. Maybe next week we can. . . ."

"No," Tony said, and pushed his fingers more deeply into her hair. "Next week you won't want to either."

Melody inhaled and was about to say something—perhaps say it softly, perhaps make some kind of offer—when the fucking door-bell rang.

He let his hand drop. He sneered. "I'll get it," he said.

It was the fat one.

"The girls are around back," Tony said pleasantly enough, and then he shut the door.

"You could have invited her in," Melody said when he got back into the kitchen. She was latching the dishwasher with one hand and the other hand had found its way to her hip. In the few seconds since he'd left, everything had changed.

"Why would I have invited her in?" Tony asked.

"Because she's the mother of one of our daughter's friends."

"Well," Tony said, heart pounding hard at the tone of her voice, "excuse the hell out of me."

Melody flushed. He could even see the blood splashed on her chest, just above her breasts. When the dishwasher was safely locked behind her, she clipped past him out the kitchen door, headed, apparently, for the dining room table where the girls' hot-dogs were still half-eaten and moldering on their Barbie Birthday plates. But before she crossed the threshold, Tony grabbed her arm, hard, without realizing *how* hard until he saw the look on her face, the quick surprised flash of pain.

"*Don't touch me,*" she hissed.

But he couldn't help it. He yanked the arm harder, and Melody stumbled into him. What looked like tears started up in her eyes, but they might just have been stinging from the pain, or dilated in the bright kitchen light, or narrowed to glare at him. She pulled away, but when he just held on tighter she whimpered a little and went limp.

"I want to talk," he said, close to her face.

There was a smell females had when they were scared, and she had it. Some kind of adrenaline. He'd smelled it on Melody before—beside him at the doctor's office when they'd been told that she was pregnant, once when they were broadsided by a sports

car at an intersection downtown. He'd smelled it before that on his
mother on a plane during turbulence, on Amy Malone beside him
on the roller coaster at Cedar Point. And he'd smelled it on his sister when he tried to give her mouth-to-mouth resuscitation on the
Vandermulen's back lawn the night after her high school graduation
when, one minute, she'd been drinking a beer on the sloped roof of
the Vandermulen's house with her boyfriend Mick, and the next she
was lying on that lawn.

Tony himself had been drinking a beer, staring at the sky. Someone
had car doors open and a stereo blasting "Stairway to Heaven" into
the twilight while a low plane's red eye blinked slowly across their
suburb. He was so stoned that the guy he was joking around with on
the patio seemed to be speaking to him without moving his mouth
when he said, "Your sister's on the roof, man," and Tony Harmon
said, "Cool," and when he looked up he could see that his sister was
rowing her arms in the air.

Wow, he'd thought, his sister was going to fly, she was going to
fucking fly right off the roof. *Cool.*

"Talk," Melody said. "Just hurry up and talk."

"I'll take my time," he said.

And then the doorbell rang again, so loud this time he dropped
her arm without intending to, and Melody hurried away from him
toward the door. One of the dining room chairs was knocked over
on its side when she bumped into it, and it fell with a dull empty
sound onto the carpet, hardly a sound at all.

It wasn't a tackle, exactly, just one arm around her waist, but
Melody had been moving fast and the force of his intercepting her
caused her to stumble over his arm to her knees. When she tried to
get to her feet again he had to throw his weight into it to keep her
down.

"Let me up!" she yelled, too loud. They were only yards from the
front door, and some girl's mother was standing just on the other
side of it, so Tony Harmon put his hand over his wife's mouth and
pushed her into the carpet. They lay like that for quite a while.
The doorbell rang one more time, and then he heard voices. Must

have been the fat one again. "The girls are around back," someone said, and then there was the sound of another car pulling into the driveway.

Melody was panting, furious, but if she'd really wanted to she could have bitten his hand, the one covering her mouth, and she didn't. He felt grateful and a little sad, somehow, that she didn't. He stood up then and pulled her to her feet, and when he said, "Get upstairs and stay there or I'm going to make a scene nobody around here will ever forget," it almost made him weep, the way she did it, the little slumping resignation of her thin shoulders, as if he'd said it in such a way she wouldn't dream of refusing.

Had he?

One of the earrings had fallen off and it lay near the toe of his shoe on the carpet. He picked it up and handed it to her and said, "I'll be right up."

Tony stepped outside, where the attractive one and the fat one were standing in exactly the same attitude in which he'd first encountered them, though now they were in the backyard instead of the driveway. The girls were still running around in some kind of choreographed chaos that must have been a game, the rules of which they'd internalized. "Oh, hi there," the attractive one said. "Must have been a good party, I guess."

"Yeah," Tony said, nodding and finding himself better able to smile casually than he had been a few hours before. He put his hands in his pockets in what he thought would appear to be a fatherly and ordinary manner. "I think the girls burned off some energy. Ate a lot of cake."

"Oh, that's great," the fat one said. "Thanks for having them."

"Hey," he said, "thanks for bringing them. My daughter made out like a bandit." Tony nodded in the direction of the laundry basket full of presents she'd ripped into before they'd lit the candles on her cake. "Oh," he said as if he'd just remembered something. "You know, I wanted to ask you if it might be possible to send my daughter off for a sleepover with one of yours tonight. Melody and I have some, well—stuff to iron out, and. . . ." Both women began to nod gravely and pleasantly at the same time, confirming what he'd known all along, that they were privy to every detail of his marital troubles.

"Oh, she's *welcome* to come with us," the attractive one said.

"Well," the fat one said, "as a matter of fact, we were going to invite any of the girls who wanted—"

"That would be great," Tony said, shaking his head and sighing. "That would help so much."

"Well, why doesn't she just come home with us now. The girls can take a swim in our pool, and then—"

"If I picked her up about, say, ten o'clock tomorrow morning, would that—?"

"She can just spend the day, too, if she wants to!"

Tony Harmon called his daughter over and told her the plan, and her reaction was simply to hop up and down on one foot cheering.

"I'll go inside and ask Melody to get a few things for her," Tony said. "You know, jammies, toothpaste."

The matrons were all smiles. A few more just like them found their ways into the backyard ("Oh, here you are. I rang the doorbell—") and each shook his hand heartily and then stood uneasily in his backyard, watching the girls dash around shouting unintelligible words at one another. *Beetleblood. Askmedoodle.* Everyone commented on the heat, but no one said a word about the humming of the electrical lines until Tony finally insisted that they all stop and listen.

"Listen," he said, holding up a hand. "It's there. It's terrible. You've just gotten used to it."

Three or four matrons cocked their ears to the sky, and Tony could see the sound of it register on their faces. Oh, yes, they agreed, that high whine, that incessant buzzing. Really, it *was* something.

And, now, as if in response to being heard, the sound swung and surged, widened and narrowed. It was the sound he imagined some-one being electrocuted would hear. Wires and heat penetrating a brain in waves. Excruciating. But numbing. And Tony felt good. He'd gotten them to stop, to listen. Even the little girls had begun to gather around, and were silent now, intent, their faces turned up to it, all of them hearing it—the daughters and their mothers looking from the wires to the sky and then back to Tony, focusing in on him as if they could tell that he was a man at the height of his powers, a man who heard things others couldn't hear, and he felt quite sure that they'd always remember him, and that day, and the way he'd stood there listening to the lines with them, and how, then, as if calling them back to the things of this world, he'd started to talk about the weather, so casually, in his own backyard, as if nothing were the slightest bit out of the ordinary here.

Our Father

A fter our father lost his passport, we had to hide him. By then, this was easier to do than it would have been earlier, before so many other fathers had gone missing. The factory still blew its whistle—some programmed and mechanized cry that couldn't be stifled—but we never saw any fathers shuffling off to work any longer. That old, gray migration through the ashes with their lunchboxes was over. Now, it was all frantic mothers out there in the streets, trying to look pleasant but with ashes of their own on their lips and under their eyes.

When there was a knock on the door, one of us would shake him awake, tug him by the arm from the couch, and shove him into the bedroom. The other would wait until the all-clear signal (a faked sneeze) to open the door.

"Is your father home, little girl?"

"No, sir."

"Who's that sneezing back there?"

"That's just my sister, sir."

The wind seemed to move around in the mouths of these official men at our door, as if they'd been wolfing down nothing for so long they couldn't keep it from coming back out. Old newspapers seemed to blow around behind their official eyes. You could see headlines

and obituaries fluttering back there. The expressions on their faces
were like car alarms that had been screaming for days and had just
that moment gone silent. Some said it was due to the estrogen in
the water, these changes in these men's faces.

These men, we felt sure, were nobody's fathers. The actual
fathers were not wearing suits like these. They were hunched and
exhausted by exhaustion and secreted away under beds and inside
bells, as clappers too soft to make a sound.

"Well, here's my card. When he comes back—"

The card always bore a name and an eagle and a blazing bonfire
in the traditional colors of red and black.

"—he's to check in with his Official. He will of course need to
bring his passport."

His passport.

Poor Daddy.

Every time he crawled out from under the bed after one of these
visits, he was covered with dust. It clung to his face and to his arms
and back, and no one bothered to brush it off. What would have
been the point? There would just be more dust to come. There was
no one to sweep the floors now that our mother spent her long days
holding her tongue in meetings, or standing beside the conveyor
belts. Our father couldn't do the sweeping because he was busy suffering, and we were too young.

So, for years we hid our father when there was a knock at the
door, and we looked for his passport. We looked under the dustbin
and in the ashes and beneath the piles of gray rags that had been
left to rot in the kitchen cupboards since our mother had started her
new job and we ate nothing but bread and peanut butter.

We couldn't find it.

"Dad, God, where did you have it last?"

He shrugged. He wiped his eyes. He said, "I'm so sorry, girls.
That's just how I am. You know your old dad. His keys. His glasses."

"But this isn't *keys*, Dad. This isn't *glasses*. This is the only proof
of your existence we *have*."

And then they sent our mother to the War, where she was killed
in an ambush within a few hours of stepping onto foreign soil. A

group of terrorist-mothers had laid in wait at a train station. We were heartbroken, but at least we knew we weren't alone. We saw the other children's mothers also lain out in a row on what looked like a filthy floor, dirty sheets over their faces, their shoes looking as new as our mother's had the day before she left for the War.

Since we had no proof of a father, we received our Orphan Benefit packages every third Saturday in a box. Tissues. Rice. Bottled water.

Our father lost his sense of humor about his situation soon after that. The rags spilled out of the cupboards, onto the floor. We didn't even know where they were coming from, the rags. They looked like used bandages—not bloody, just sooty. They were dingy and good for nothing except covering up our father, who was completely camouflaged there on the gray couch under the gray rags.

Soon, we received our notices to report to the Division in which our mother had worked before she was drafted. In a way, it was a relief, getting out of there during the day. Even when the boss was in a bad mood she'd let us joke around with each other. And there were a lot of jokes. So many women standing around a conveyor belt all day—you can imagine.

Then, after a few years, they declared amnesty for all the fathers who'd lost their passports. The President said she couldn't think of any reason to go on punishing such long-forgotten mishaps. Fathers were absentminded. It was time we just admitted it, got on with our lives.

But we didn't tell our father about the amnesty. What difference would it have made? It might have made him actually feel worse. So we let him go on thinking he was in danger. Sometimes one of us would pretend to knock officially on the door so the other could pretend to hurry him into hiding. It got harder and harder to get him off the couch and then back out from under the bed, so we didn't do it very often. Just often enough. Things went on quite well like this for quite a long time.

Surely, we thought, they wouldn't send us both to the War, being that we were orphans, as far as they knew—but, why wouldn't they, of course?

Somebody's Mistress, Somebody's Wife

Often she unplugged the answering machine and let the phone ring sixteen, seventeen, times before she answered it. It was always him. He was the only one who would let the phone ring that long. He was the only one who called her in the morning while she was getting ready for work.

"*Babe*," he'd say, as if he were out of breath, but not as if she'd surprised him by answering.

"What do you want?" she'd ask.

To this, he'd say nothing. She pictured him in his little white sports car with the roof down, his silver hair gleaming in the sunlight, his red tie lapping the wind over his shoulder, his cell phone held to an ear, maybe one elbow resting on the car door, arm extended, driving with his knee as he sometimes liked to do.

Even in the winter she pictured this, although he lived even farther north than she did, and the winter was a bad one.

"Don't call me again, Conrad," she'd say. But then she'd hold the phone to her ear a long time, listening to him breathe, waiting for him to say something he never got around to saying.

When Karen was a child she'd been told a cautionary urban legend by her grandmother about a man who'd rested his elbow on the open window of his car, and it had been lopped off by a passing station wagon—torn right off at the shoulder. The man had driven ten more miles without realizing his arm was gone, until he was pulled over by a policeman who'd noticed the blood pouring out of the man's car, painting a red stripe down the middle of the road.

Karen sometimes imagined Conrad driving down the freeway with one arm ripped from the socket, his gray suit in bloody tatters at the shoulder as he held the phone to his ear with his free hand.

Sometimes she pictured herself in the passenger seat beside him, lifting a hand to wave to a passing child on a bicycle, and suddenly realizing that her own arm was just a gushing, empty sleeve of blood.

Usually, he was the first one to hang up.

It had been a year since Karen broke things off with Conrad. It was hard to believe she'd once been that woman standing in a hotel parking lot while the rain poured down on her in a Hollywood-like deluge—nearly drowning in her own hair, which was running with water and plastered to her face. She was screaming up at the window of their room. Every time she inhaled, her mouth filled with water and hair. It was the middle of the night. She always suspected that Conrad was, himself, the one who called the cops, but all she knew was that she was guided into the back of the patrol car and told to hush up by a weary-looking uniformed officer, who said, "Jesus. People are trying to sleep in there lady. What is this, some kind of love trouble?"

She didn't bother to explain.

The cop said, "Look, just get out of here, okay. If I have to come back here, it's going to be Disturbing the Peace, okay. Trust me, you don't want to spend the night in jail."

The officer came around the side of the car then and opened it for her like a gentleman—a gentleman who was opening the door for her because there were no handles in the back of his patrol car for her to open it herself, ushering her out into the parking lot into a driving rainstorm.

Karen had no illusions that night. She knew she looked like a drowned rat, as her grandmother used to say. She knew that if this police officer felt anything other than contempt for her, it was pity.

Soon after, she moved eighty miles south, and got a good, new job. She bought a bungalow in a funky little neighborhood full of bungalows. If he didn't call her in the mornings, maybe she would have forgotten Conrad entirely by now.

Conrad and his wife of twenty-two years.

Conrad and his mansion on the lake.

Conrad and his missing toes, which had fallen off on Mount Everest, and the way her own toes felt as she slid her foot across the bed and ran them over his toes, those little bubblish stumps. Conrad always pretended to be ashamed of his toeless foot, but he never missed a chance to point it out to her, or make a big show of stuffing wadded gauze into his shoe before he put it on.

"Morning," Jim Porter said when she reached the entrance to her office building. He was reading the paper with his legs spread wide apart on the bench outside the office. He didn't look up when he greeted her.

Karen had found out a few months before, through interoffice rumors, that Jim's sister, when he was a little boy and the sister was thirteen, had stolen their father's car and driven it off a bridge into a river. She was considered a Missing Person for four months before the car rose to the surface of the river with Jim's sister still at the wheel.

"He's never gotten over it," Melissa whispered.

Indeed, it seemed like the kind of thing one would never get over, a dark detail, a kind of grainy shadow that would trail Jim everywhere—but in truth Karen saw no signs that he hadn't gotten over it. He made a lot of crude jokes around the coffee pot. He spent a lot of time on the Internet, looking for antique letter openers for sale on eBay. Karen tried to imagine, if it had been her own sister, would *she* have gotten over it?

Probably.

Her own sister had been a kind of Missing Person for the last two decades of Karen's life, ever since their mother had died and Marybeth had accused Karen of usurping her affections at the deathbed. ("It was like I wasn't even there!" Marybeth screamed in the hospital parking lot. "Like she was looking at you the whole time she was dying, like I wasn't even in the fucking room!")

It was easy enough to imagine her sister at thirteen, swimming trapped in a stolen car, maybe trying lethargically to unbuckle her seat belt and get out, hoping for a while, and then dreaming, the way those whose brains are being deprived of oxygen must dream—dim light and echoes and empty corridors—until what Marybeth had been to Karen collapsed in on itself until it was smaller than a pencil eraser, and then the head of a pin, and then less than a pin-prick where once a very bitter older sister had been.

It was perfect summer weather. The clouds looked artistically arranged in the sky. That weekend Karen had planted impatiens in a circle around the trees in her front yard. They looked like Christmas lights burning there in the middle of the day, electrically red and white.

The bungalow next to hers had been for sale for months, and finally someone had bought it and was moving in. Karen had to admit to herself a bit of disappointment when she saw who it was—another woman in her thirties, also single—although she would not have admitted to herself that she was hoping for a single man. Or even a married man.

"Hey!" the new neighbor had called over from an open window after her moving van pulled away. "I like your house!"

It was a joke everyone on the block made, since all the bungalows on the block were the same.

"Ha! Ha!" Karen said, trying to make it sound like laughter.

It turned out that the new woman next door was freshly divorced. She'd lost everything in the divorce, including custody of her nine-year-old daughter. When Karen stopped in on Sunday to bring her a plate of brownies, it seemed that all this new neighbor had brought with her to unpack were about a hundred framed photographs of the daughter.

Her daughter's name was Beth. The new neighbor's name was Elizabeth.

Elizabeth made some instant iced tea, and she and Karen sat together on the couch, which was the only piece of furniture in the bungalow. Elizabeth wound her limbs around her as if she were made of rubber. Outside, there was the sound of an ice-cream truck playing tinny children's music. Elizabeth put her face in her hands and began to weep.

"Oh, God," Karen said, and patted the woman's shoulder. "I'm so sorry. Would you like me to go?"

Elizabeth shook her head *no no*. Her hair was a mass of dark curls. She'd told Karen that she was from Russia, although there was no trace of an accent in her heavily Midwestern-sounding English.

"It's why they took my daughter," she said. "Because I'm not American. I have no rights in this country. They can do whatever they want to me. My ex-husband is a powerful man. He *runs* the government."

Karen couldn't imagine what the woman meant. Was she trying to say that her ex-husband was the *President?* That seemed unlikely. But by some horrible coincidence then the ice-cream truck pulled up at the curb right outside the new neighbor's house and kept the music—"I'm a Little Teapot"—blaring as children yelped and cried out, surrounding the truck.

Elizabeth wept harder—longer, rasping, ragged inhalations followed by shuddering gulps. "I can't help it, but I have to," Elizabeth said. "Everything will always remind me of her. I'll never get over this."

"Can't your daughter visit?" Karen asked. "Can't you visit your daughter?

Elizabeth shook her head vehemently. "He's guaranteed that I'll never see her again."

A straggly little black dog came running out of the bedroom then, skidding and slipping across the wooden floors on its toenails before leaping into Elizabeth's lap. She buried her face in its greasy-looking fur, and said, "I'll visit you tomorrow, Kathy. I need to be alone now."

She was going to remind her that her name was Karen, not Kathy, but thought better of it.

The people at Karen's office were chatty, and immature. Very little was accomplished on any given day, but often just before a presentation or a meeting there would be a surge of frantic energy that resulted in screaming fights, and tearful reconciliations. Karen tried to steer clear of most of her coworkers, and just do her job, but Melissa was always trying to drag her into office politics and gossip. Melissa hated everyone they worked with, but she was always urging Karen to join them for lunches or for drinks after work.

One mind-numbingly dull afternoon, Karen confided in Melissa about Conrad and immediately wished she hadn't.

"God," Melissa said. "What an asshole."

"I don't know," Karen said, feeling oddly defensive of Conrad. "There were never any promises made. I knew what I was getting into. I knew he was married. I just didn't know how deeply in love I would fall."

"I don't mean about *you*. I was thinking of his *wife*. Did she ever suspect?"

"I don't know," Karen said, bristling. She did not want to think about Conrad's wife. What did she care about Conrad's *wife*. It seemed rude of Melissa to ask. "I never met his wife."

"Well," Melissa said. "I knew someone once whose aunt suspected that her husband was having an affair, and this aunt worked in a factory, and she had access to radioactive materials, and she started mailing it to the woman her husband was having an affair with—just a bit here and there in envelopes that looked like, you know, coupons and such. And the mistress had no idea what was happening, but her hair started falling out, and her fingernails were peeling off, and then one night she woke up to go to the bathroom and saw herself in the dark in the medicine chest mirror, and she was *glowing*."

Karen went to the trash can and threw her styrofoam up into it. "I need to get back to work," she said.

"But do you think, you know, his wife would ever—?"

"Conrad's wife doesn't work in a factory," Karen said. "Conrad is one of the richest men in this state."

Melissa shrugged.

The new neighbor's dog was named Buttons. It never barked, but it would run out the neighbor's back door every time she opened it, and come panting into Karen's yard, where it would head straight for the impatiens, and, after pissing on them, begin digging them up. Karen would come out on her front stoop with her arms crossed, and watch. Elizabeth would just stand there, too, smiling sadly across the narrow stretch of grass and dandelions between them. If she understood that her dog was digging up something Karen had planted, and wanted, she didn't register any problem with that.

One Saturday morning while Buttons pissed on the impatiens, a beautiful emerald and blue butterfly rose out of the shrubbery under Karen's bedroom window and began to make its way shakily on the breeze across her yard. It glowed as if it were bearing some sort of radioactive material on its wings, shimmering and powdery and dazzling. When Buttons saw it, he put down his leg, and tore after it, leaping into the air, snapping it off the breeze in one bite.

Karen looked over at Elizabeth, who was dragging on a cigarette now, looking, if anything, pleased with her pet.

"Buttons belonged to my daughter. My ex-husband hates animals. He made me take Buttons with me when I left, said he'd skin him in front of our daughter if I didn't," she told Karen, who was careful not to press the issue—any of the issues. "Kathy," she said. "You have no idea what I've been through."

Conrad had always brought her unusual presents when they had their trysts. A pomegranate. A branch of apple blossoms. A praying mantis. He was a very rich man. He could have given her diamonds, he said. But diamonds were dull. Diamonds were what any rich man would have thought to give his mistress. Conrad was not just a businessman. He was creative.

In truth, Karen wouldn't have minded diamonds. She *wasn't* rich. The praying mantis refused to fly away when she opened her bedroom window and let it go free. It sat on her windowsill praying, creepy little heart-shaped head bowed, for days before it fell off, drifting the ten stories down to the street where Karen hoped it got run over. The only jewelry he ever gave her was a hemp bracelet he had braided himself. At the center of it he'd tied a toenail, one of his own, on which he'd painstakingly painted the silhouette of the summit of Mount Everest against a light blue sky.

"It's one of a kind," he said. "There's not another bracelet like this in the world."

She never asked him where the other four toenails had gone.

Maybe she didn't want to know.

He told her about his wife, who had Irritable Bowel Syndrome and had been unwilling to make love to him for the last twenty-two years of their marriage. But also about his beautiful daughters. Blond, athletic, musical, academically-gifted girls. And also his one son, who caused Conrad so much grief he really didn't want to get into it.

When Karen made the ultimatum every mistress eventually makes, Conrad blamed his inability to leave his wife on the son. "He's been diagnosed with clinical depression."

"So have I!" Karen said.

"Karen, darling," Conrad said, holding up his hands as if to prove that he had all his digits.

"What is it?" Karen asked when she stepped into the office and saw them all there, standing around the coffee pot, staring into it as the black water dripped into it one scalding drop at a time.

Melissa looked up.

"It's Jim," she said.

"What about Jim?"

"You won't believe it," Melissa said.

"Try me," Karen said.

"He went home to visit his parents for the weekend. He was driving back here on Sunday, along the river. A little girl on a bicycle rolled down her driveway into the street right in front of him. He swerved to miss her, and drove off the road, into the river, at the *exact spot* where his sister drove into the river *fifteen years ago to the day*."

"No way," Karen said.

Her other five office mates looked up, nodding their heads as if against unusually powerful gravity.

"I have great news!" Elizabeth shouted across their yards as Buttons, crouching among the impatiens, strained irritably to have a bowel movement. "My husband is letting me see my daughter this weekend!"

"Great!" Karen said.

"Kathy, do you know how much this means to me?"

Karen had never had any particular interest in having children, but she supposed she could imagine the excitement of seeing the daughter you'd thought you'd never see again if she tried. She was, however, distracted by Buttons, and Buttons' business among her impatiens.

"Can you do me a favor?"

"I suppose," Karen said. "What is it?"

"Can you watch Buttons this weekend? While I visit with my daughter?"

Conrad's wife found a number on her husband's cell phone statement, a number he'd dialed every weekday morning of that month, a call lasting, each time, one or two minutes.

Curious, Conrad's wife dialed it herself.

After seventeen rings, a woman answered.

Conrad's wife held the phone to her ear and listened to the very crisp space between them, frozen in her bare feet in the kitchen, staring out the French doors to the backyard where two squirrels were chasing each other around in manic circles. The woman on the other end of the line sounded to Conrad's wife as if she were, perhaps, applying makeup, or tidying up a bedroom. Some sort of animal was making a muffled whiny noise in the background, it seemed. After a minute or two passed, the woman on the other end of the line said, "Don't call me anymore, Conrad. It's over between us."

Conrad's wife called information after that, and was given the address of the house where the phone bill for the number she'd dialed was sent. She jotted it down on a piece of paper, but she was upset, distracted, a bit dyslexic, and reversed the last two digits of the house number when she did.

What choice did Karen have but to keep the little dog after Elizabeth never returned from the weekend with her daughter? It was months before they found the poor woman's body cut into small pieces and stuffed into the toilet tank and the crawl space of her bungalow—which was only inspected some months after the new couple moved in and complained to the realtor who'd sold it to them about the plumbing and the stench—and a huge, protracted courtroom drama full of shouting and paparazzi and Special Reports interrupting every television show Karen tried to watch for many months before Elizabeth's ex-husband, who happened to be the Chairman of the Federal Reserve Board, was convicted of her murder.

Buttons learned some tricks. Fetch. Sit. Beg. He slept for the first few weeks at the foot of Karen's bed, but when she allowed it, he liked to make his way up to the pillow beside hers and curl against her face.

A kind of love blossomed between them, like the love between a mother and her child, perhaps—especially after the accident and the months of recuperation that followed, when Buttons was Karen's only source of affection and companionship after her sister, who'd returned to Karen's life to nurse her back to health had died when her cell phone exploded in her hand, killing her instantly in front of the elementary school where the children had just run out the front doors to be greeted by their parents, and the ten million pieces of Karen's sister's carnage rained down on them as they screamed.

Now, every spring, Karen planted impatiens for Buttons just so he could dig them up.

It was difficult learning to adjust to life with only one arm after so many years of having two, but Buttons was a great help to Karen. Bringing the mail to her. Licking the tears from her cheeks. Somewhere, she knew, some other woman was driving for hundreds of miles with Karen's arm embedded in the grill of her car. She'd find it someday, and never know whose it was, or where it had come from.

Probably, she was Conrad's wife. Probably, Conrad would recognize the arm as Karen's as soon as he saw the hemp bracelet he had braided for her and his own toenail at the center of it, and have a heart attack, dying in their driveway in front of their home, surrounded by his screaming daughters and his wife. His son would hang himself in the public park, but, it being Halloween weekend, he would be taken simply for a macabre decoration for several days.

It would not be until many years later that Karen would begin to realize how selfish she had been, having an affair with a married man. The chain of events it might have begun. How little she'd known then of love, she realized. And family. The humble, hopeful vows people took to get themselves through this life intact. How a betrayal, even of a stranger, was like a tiny spot of rust that eventually ate away everything. The vast lacy decay spreading its terrible veil clear across the country. She'd been a tourist back then, taking nothing in, giving nothing back. Who was left to whom she could confess? Who was left to offer forgiveness? Who would she be in the universe, when her soul was sucked back up into it, without this?

It wouldn't be for another decade that Buttons, grown elderly on the pillow beside hers, would need to be taken to the veterinarian. By then, two new couples had come and gone from the bungalow next door. They'd moved out when pieces of Elizabeth continued to surface at random intervals in their toilet bowl. Her only friend back at the office, Melissa, had been swallowed by a sink hole that no one but a few corrupt developers were aware lay just beneath the parking lot of the shopping mall, waiting to swallow someone.

"Buttons hasn't eaten for days," Karen said, handing him over to the veterinarian with her one arm. "Can you help him, Doctor? Buttons is a good little dog. He's never hurt a soul."

The veterinarian looked at Buttons for a few seconds, and then he looked up at Karen. He cleared his throat. He said, "Ma'am, I don't know how to tell you this, but—Buttons—Buttons isn't a dog."

Outside the veternarian's office, Karen heard the familiar, tinny music of the ice-cream truck, and then the squealing of brakes, and then a child's shriek cut off abruptly, as if the shriek itself had been yanked out of the child's mouth and stuffed into a pocket.

The child's own father, as it happened, was driving that ice-cream truck when his only son dashed in front of it.

Karen nodded sadly, feeling the tears gather in the corners of her eyes, but also feeling swollen with wonder at this strange life and her own role in it, full of a kind of regret that was also a kind of genuine awe, before she said to the veterinarian, "I know."

Joyride

"H ey," my dad said, tossing the keys onto the couch beside me, "why not take the old family convertible for a joyride, pal?"

He wasn't joking, but it wasn't what he wanted to say, either. What he really wanted to say was that it bothered him to see me sitting on the couch with a copy of *National Geographic* on a sunny Saturday afternoon.

When I was younger, he used to say, "Hey, pal, why don't you go outside and throw rocks at birds, like all the other red-blooded American boys?"

And maybe he didn't really mean *go throw rocks at birds*, but, instead, *I'm not sure I like you*, or, *I'm frightened that I don't like you*—and still he would have been happy if I'd done it. Thrown rocks at birds. It would have proven something about me, and it would also have given him the excuse he'd been looking for all my life to spank me, or deck me. To teach me a lesson.

Mom walked through the room then with a smile that showed all her teeth, even the back molars. Sometimes she might smile that way and say, "Oh, Jim, leave the boy alone!" But today she was trying hard to have a Good Weekend, and didn't want to provoke him, so she only smiled.

"Okay, Dad," I said, and picked up the keys.

I put down the *National Geographic*, walked past him, across the living room, out the front door.

It was summer. Everything was green. The green that a shard of an old Coke bottle turns after a long time in the sea. Or something equally green. Maybe even something twice as green. My father had already taken the roof down. I pulled his convertible into the street.

Grandma was asleep when I got there. She was in her chair, but leaning forward, draped over the tray attached to her wheelchair like a rag doll. Her roommate was lying so still on the opposite bed that she looked completely dead. Her eyes were open. When I walked past her, she chuckled. Her name was Eve L. Mason, and it was like a cold trickle of pure evil, that laughter, and I was careful not to turn around and look at her. Once, when I was much younger and my grandmother was new to the nursing home, Eve L. had whispered something to me. My father had been wheeling my grandmother around in the hallway. I couldn't hear what Eve L. was whispering. She indicated with a few bony fingers that I should come over to the side of the bed. She whispered again, and I still couldn't hear her, so I leaned down, and she sprang up and grabbed me by the ears and pulled my face to hers, cackling. Her breath smelled like a trashcan full of old leaves that have gotten wet. Night after night after that I dreamed of Eve L. pulling me down, down, down into dead leaves. "Just ignore her," my father had said.

"Grandma?"

I touched the back of her head. Her white hair was so tenuous and brittle, but long and floating about her head in wild wisps, that it was like air that had calcified. As if shallow breaths had risen and stiffened in frayed strands around my grandmother's head.

She lifted her face but didn't open her eyes.

How, I thought, looking at her eyelids, could such thin lids keep the light out.

For a frightening second I thought she might have been looking at me *through* them.

"It's me," I said. "Grandma. It's Mark."

The eyelids sprang open.

She blinked away the milk—six, seven, eight times—and then she smiled.

I knew, looking at her, that anyone who didn't know her would probably fail to register the smile as a smile. As pleasure. As *joy*. What they'd see instead was the wrecked body around the smile. The misery of her old age. The blindness.

But, if you knew her, you'd see that she was incredibly happy to see me.

A few months earlier, I'd taken Hilary Agnew to the prom. She'd been the one who asked me—shoved a piece of paper across the biology lab table that said, "Mark. Would you like to go to the prom with me? Hilary."

I had no way of knowing for sure, but my feeling was that some friend of Hilary's might have written that note. If Hilary had any friends. Or maybe an older sister, or her mother. When I saw her in the hall later, and said, trying to smile politely, "Sure, Hilary," she'd only shrugged, bitten her quivering bottom lip, her eyebrows also trembling, as if she might cry, as if I'd agreed to attend her funeral.

But she'd worn an amazing dress.

There were layers and layers of satin involved in that dress, and, under the satin, there seemed to be lace. It was a pale purple, with straps that held it elaborately around her chest and neck, and then crisscrossed in a dizzying ladder down her bare back.

It would have been easy to see only that dress. The frivolous, girlish, ecstasy of that. But, if you looked closer, what you saw at the center of all that—Hilary—was still a small, depressed girl with mascara smeared under one of her eyes. She drooped in the dress beside me in her parents' living room while her mother grimly took pictures. She dropped in the dress in my father's car beside me.

When we pulled up to the high school, I turned the keys off in the ignition and said, "Hilary? Is this what you want to do?"

She looked down at her elaborate lap.

After what seemed like a very long time, she shook her head, and a tear fell off her face, disappearing in the satin.

"Is there—anything wrong?" I asked.

So quietly I almost couldn't hear her, she said, "No."

Her mother was standing on the front porch when I brought Hilary home.

The expression on Mrs. Agnew's face, even before she could have recognized who it was pulling into her long, winding drive, did not betray the slightest shred of surprise.

"Grandma. Want to go for a ride?"

Behind us, Eve L. parroted me in a nasty little voice, "*Grandma want to go for a ride?*"

My grandmother slapped her knee with her curled and rigid hand, and said, "Yes, I, do."

I took the tray off her chair and put it on the floor, and pushed my grandmother past Eve L. into the hallway and down the long, whimpering corridor to the front door, and then out into the bright sunshine.

The nurses and aides at the front desk did not seem to notice us leave, or, if they noticed, they apparently did not feel it was any of their concern.

My father's car was the only one in the lot. I wheeled my grandmother to the passenger side, and opened it. I scooped her out (she was as light as a skeleton—a skeleton in a polyester dress) and set her down in the seat. When I leaned across her to buckle her belt, she giggled. I didn't know what to do with the wheelchair, so I left it sitting empty in the parking lot. The sky was clear, and who would steal a wheelchair.

Anyway, at that time, I thought we would only go for a short drive, and be right back.

———

In a few years, I would be a sophomore in college, and a girl I'd had a crush on for a year would come stumbling down the hallway of our dorm with a bottle of Wild Turkey in her hand.

Her long, dark hair was a mess, and her lips looked engorged, so red they looked like a wound more than an orifice.

She'd stumble and fall to her knees right in front of the open door of my room, look up, and slur, "I know you always want to fuck me. It's okay to fuck me."

I would stand up.

I would go to her.

I would lift her up and carry her, as light as my grandmother, but less alive, and put her down on my roommate's lower bunk.

With one hand, she would bring the Wild Turkey to her lips and slug hard from it, and with the other, she would unbutton her blouse. I would sit at the edge of the bed, and as she rubbed her hand on my crotch, I would close my eyes, and what I would see was the way the wind blowing through the open roof of my father's car had lifted my grandmother's white hair, and placed it down again carefully on her shoulders. How she'd tilted her head back and opened her mouth to the sky.

The Foreclosure

This happened during one of those terrible months when my life was purely about jealousy. Jealousy, envy, resentment, spite. I woke up every morning tangled in them like barbed wire. I lay down to sleep in a prickling gown of them every night. I woke up angry and tired.

I hadn't always been that way. There'd been a time in my life when I would never have believed you if you'd told me how consumed a person might become with the desire for a *thing,* and that I might become such a person. Men, I'd wanted. A sense of accomplishment. Recognition for the talents I'd imagined I had. I'd even occasionally longed to feel the solid perfumed weight of a baby against my chest. During the dead months of winter, I'd craved the sun. During the long hot months of summer and pavement I'd dreamed of ocean breezes. But I'd never pined, as I was pining in those months, for a *thing.*

I had been raised by frugal parents who never spoke about money. We never had much, but there was always enough. I never heard my parents argue about how to pay a bill or if one of them had spent too much on something. They never mentioned how I might make money myself someday. When I said I wanted to be a poet, that I was marrying a painter, they gave us their blessing, and then they died. My mother's cancer followed my father's heart attack. There was no inheritance, but there was no debt. It was as if they'd taken care to sweep the floor behind them, moving backward out the door so as to leave not a trace of themselves when they left.

Before we married, my husband and I used to say that we would be happy in a shoebox together. A shoebox next to some railroad tracks. A damp shoebox. Some newspaper for our bed. We would lie beside one another in the sweaty rumpled twin bed in my apartment and describe the awful squalor in which we knew we could find complete contentment. A shoebox shared with a shoeboxful of mice.

But then we lived for five years together in an apartment with thin walls, patchy carpet, neighbors above and below us who stomped and shouted at one another and played music only they could appreciate so loudly we could recite the lyrics to their grating songs. The pets they were not supposed to have in their apartments would yowl and bark and whine through the nights when they weren't home, and then yap and meow with pitiful relief when they returned, slamming the doors behind them, cracking open the tabs on their beer and soda cans. When a truck drove through the street, it shook the whole building so completely you could really understand that the building was made of plywood, sawdust, nothing, and a few slaps of diluted off-white paint over it all. The water in the shower smelled like moldy cheese if you didn't run it long enough, and if you ran it too long it was stone cold by the time you stepped in.

My husband and I both worked long days in cubicles to pay the rent, and some months we had to appeal to the landlord to give us an extra week. The landlord would wait until after he thought I was out of earshot to say to my husband, "You pay me on time, or I throw you out."

It was during this period of time that more and more people were getting thrown out. Of their apartments. Their jobs. Their houses. Some of the women I worked with talked about how lucky they felt to have their jobs, or their husbands, or their cars. They were just trying to hang on. But others seemed poised to take advantage of the situation. They talked about the sinking economy, and the tanking of the job market. They'd say things like, "We're going to wait just a few more months, and then we're going to snap up a house. People are getting desperate. Soon you'll be able to buy yourself a mansion for a song."

I could not, myself, imagine such a song. The song of our bank account was always hovering just under three hundred dollars. The song of our gas tank was always a quarter of a tank. What would such a song sound like? Could it afford lyrics, or would it be played on some kind of wind instrument?

No.

No instrument.

Just wind.

I neither felt thankful for what I had nor hopeful that anything better could be had because others were losing what they'd once had. My husband never spoke about *making art*, as he used to call it. I wrote no poetry.

It was during this time that I began to get up early to walk through the surrounding neighborhoods on the weekends while my husband was still asleep. I would walk quickly so that I could get as far away from our block as I could, as quickly as possible. Our block and the ones surrounding it were renters' blocks, seeming always to be overhung with gray clouds, as if the clouds had gathered on purpose over our rooftops because we couldn't afford blue sky.

Our blocks were immediately adjacent to blocks that also looked temporary, but not as temporary as ours. There were houses, at least. Boxy houses, some of them divided into two or three residences. Duplexes. Triplexes. Close to bus stops. Convenient to convenience stores, where people like my husband and I bought canned soups and packaged bread at outrageous prices because we didn't want to have to put gas in the car to get us to the cheaper stores. But there were signs of a slightly more permanent life on those blocks. There would be an occasional bike locked to a mailbox out front, or a plastic pool that hadn't been used in years.

Beyond this neighborhood, there were a few blocks of houses that had once been owned, it seemed, by people who'd lived in them for many years and taken good care of them but were now being rented out to strangers, or to relatives down on their luck. Screen doors that wouldn't close properly might be blowing around in the wind. Garbage cans no one bothered to bring in waited at the end of the driveway. But there was a dignity under it. Hollyhocks that might have been planted decades earlier, tended back then, were still blooming here and there along a weathered fence.

These neighborhoods were preferable to ours, but not by much. It was *past* these neighborhoods where I found my heartache. The farther I walked, the more I discovered to long for, and to admire, and to despise.

Each of these mornings, I tried to take a different route, discover a new little pocket of unbearable, unattainable beauty: Little brick bungalows. Light-blue clapboard. Porches with rocking chairs. Windowboxes stuffed with foliage. Here, in these distant neighborhoods, it was late spring the way late spring was meant to be. The weather was glorious, as if choreographed for flowers. Blue sky. Swirling clouds. The grass was so green it looked as if it might shatter if you stepped on it.

I would not look directly at the houses I passed. I would glance at them furtively, sidelong, and will myself not to stop, not to stare.

Still, with each one I passed, I stole a little something. The petunias along the walk. The trellis, and the pink roses climbing it. An overgrown shrub. A welcome mat with an embroidered rooster on it near a front door. A lazy calico cat stretched out on a stoop. A few clunky notes from a piano drifting through a window. The swish of a broom sweeping dust out a side door and into a driveway.

These little treasures became mine, slipping into my imagination's pocket along with the things I couldn't see: The clawfoot tub. The porcelain knobs on the cupboard doors. The striped wallpaper in the bedroom at the end of the hall, and the way the sun spilled onto the wooden floorboards, a white-washed wall, a lacy coverlet.

I became the woman setting the kettle on the stove, waiting for the whistle, pouring herself a cup of green tea, carrying it with her out to the little fenced-in backyard, sighing with the sun on my bare arms. My laundry was softly drying itself on a line. It smelled powdery and humidly lush. Later I would run myself a salted bath in that clawfoot tub.

March turned into April, April to May, to June. In those weeks, I'd walked past hundreds of houses, and each one lodged itself inside me. Even the ugly ones. Even the ones with broken shutters or peeling paint. I could fix those up, I knew. I imagined myself on Saturday mornings hauling an aluminum ladder through the crabgrass. My husband slamming the pickets back to their runners with a hammer. *Fixin' this dump up.* I always tried, on each walk, to see a new neighborhood, but sometimes I forgot which little winding side streets I'd already been down, and I'd find myself in front of a familiar house, and have a sense of déjà vu, thinking *I once lived here,* before I realized that I'd only imagined a life there, maybe only the weekend before, so vividly that I might as well have lived it.

So, when I found myself in front the most beautiful of all the houses one Saturday in June, unable to continue walking because the feeling of recognition, and need, and familiarity, and certainty, was so great that I found I had rested my hand on the latch of the little gate of the decorative fence at the end of the walk, and that I was opening it, and stepping through it, and that my sneakers were padding along the flat stones leading up to the front porch, and then up the two cement steps, and then that I was *on* the front porch, I was less surprised by my own behavior than I might have been, than I should have been.

This was a tiny pale-green bungalow, one story, on a street called Vervain Lane. There were white shutters on the windows, lace curtains behind them. There were windowboxes spilling purple flowers. There were more purple flowers in the gardens on either side of the house. A swinging chair hung from chains to the roof of the porch, which was bordered with bric-a-brac. The front door was solid and wooden, but it had a little diamond-shaped pane in the center, and a bright brass doorknob. Before I could knock, a woman peered at me through the diamond, opened the door, and said, "Come in."

I was not overly surprised at first to be invited in so casually. I assumed she'd been expecting someone else, and had mistaken me for her. I opened my mouth to try to explain myself, to begin my apology, but the woman turned her back and said, "Sit down on the couch. I'll get you a glass of water," and then she disappeared.

I did not, of course, sit down. It would have been so rude to accept her hospitality only then to tell her that she was confused, that I was not the guest she'd been expecting. But when the woman came back out of the kitchen with the glass of water, she looked, I thought, annoyed that I was still standing, and glanced from me to the couch, as if judging the distance between us. Why had I not sat down?

She was a nice-looking woman. Maybe ten years older than I was, ten pounds heavier. Her hair was ash-blond, and although it was long and wavy, it did not look like the kind of hair a woman took pride in. It was just naturally luxurious. Accidentally lovely. Full. Healthy. Alive.

But her face was pale, tired-looking. There were girlish freckles across the bridge of her nose, but also dark circles under her gray eyes. She wasn't wearing makeup. The white dress she wore was gauzy, and on another woman—or on this one at another time—it would have looked California-hippy. Something you'd buy in an import store, smelling of patchouli. Something you'd wear to an outdoor concert on a warm summer night. But on this woman, on this weekend morning, it looked like widow's weeds.

"Please," she said. "I invited you to sit down."

I hesitated before I took the glass of water and went to her couch.

The room we were in was so beautiful, I could hardly bare it. It put a lump in my throat to look around. It made my chest ache: There was a fireplace. The brick mantel had been painted white. The couch was overstuffed. A sateen shimmer to the white cushions, the floral pillows leaning against the armrests. There was a wooden rocker on a nubby round rose-colored rug, and a gleaming oak trunk, used as a coffee table, on another circular rug—this one a little shabby, but with a forest scene, complete with lumberjack and doe and buck, woven into it.

There were no books or magazines on the trunk, or decorations on the mantlepiece, or pictures on the walls, so I projected my own things there: My husband's big glossy Brueghel book, which was presently propping open a window in our apartment, on the trunk, and a few literary journals in which, perhaps, I'd one day publish a poem or two. A gardening book. I imagined paintings my husband had done years earlier, in storage now in his brother's basement, hanging on the walls. I would arrange my dead mother's collection of antique sugar bowls on the mantel. Myself, instead of this woman in the rocker, would be saying to an unexpected guest sitting on her couch with a glass of water, "I've seen you outside the house several times—"

I was shocked, as if I'd been caught in a lie I'd yet to tell. I started to interrupt, to tell her that she was mistaken, that I'd never even been in this part of town before, and that in truth I had no idea why I'd come to her door, but she raised a hand as if to hush me before I was able to speak. "Please," she said. "It's understandable. You've heard about our trouble, and you're curious. I've watched you standing outside, staring at the windows."

"No," I said. "I've never even been in this neighborhood. Today is the first—"

She waved the hand now, and then held a finger to her lips to stop me from saying any more, shaking her head. I couldn't tell if she was trying to keep me from making more excuses for myself or if she was trying to keep someone else from hearing me, and then I heard footsteps in a room behind her. She cocked her head. She was listening, too. She took the finger from her lips, and the footsteps stopped, and then she said, "You don't need to explain."

"It's just such a lovely house," I said, explaining anyway. "It's so charming. So perfect. It takes my breath away. I live in an apartment and—"

"You'd like to live in my house."

I felt mortified when tears sprang into my eyes. To hide them from her, I looked down, into my glass of water. I brought it to my lips, took a sip from it. The taste of the water was so bright and clean, so much the taste I imagined water would have after pouring down the side of a mountain, melting straight off the icy mountaintop, that I had to will myself to swallow it, to look up again, still with that brilliance in my mouth. The sun poured through all the windows at once, as if it were at the very zenith of the sky. It shimmered in the woman's ash-blond hair, revealing a few little rivulets of paler hair, golder gold. She ran a hand through it, and the gesture seemed to tuck the sunlight behind a cloud for just a second before it sprang back out. But the look on her face was terrible—almost as if all of her had been painted with great care, by a master, in loving detail, but the face had been smudged away with a gray eraser. She said, "I would show you the house, but the bedroom, my daughter's room, they're—"

"Oh, God," I said. "No. Of course not. I didn't expect a tour. You've been more than generous, inviting me in, giving me the water. Please." I stood up, and this time when I did I heard stomping again in the room behind her, and then what sounded like a woman trying to explain something important to someone through a closed door, in a whisper, loud enough to make out a few words. *We ignored . . . and were always. . . . We actually . . . was saying. . . .*

I heard a door opening, and then a little girl in a diaper and a pink shirt came dashing into the living room, threw herself into the woman's arms, panting. The child seemed terrified, but she wasn't crying. She was completely expressionless, all blond curls and pale skin, gray eyes like her mother's, bare white arms and legs, like a package of sunlight, herself, tossed into the living room, into her mother's arms.

But, unlike her mother, the child's cheeks were radiant with life. She looked almost feverish with it, in that way of children when they've just woken from a sweaty nap. Her lips, too—rosebud red. I could smell her. The little-girlness of her. She was freshness, lake water, bread dough, moss. "Mama," the girl said, and the woman stood up quickly with the child in her arms and said to me, "I'm sorry. You need to go now," nodding to the door. "Hurry. Please."

There was no alarm in her voice, and it wasn't a rude request. It was more like the kind of command a crossing guard would make. Something suggested for your own safety. An important announcement. Nothing personal. I put the glass of water down, said a rushed thank you, opened the door, stepped out, and closed it behind me. I made my way back through the manicured garden, down the flat stones, out the gate, and latched it behind me, and walked quickly all the way back to the apartment, where my husband was still asleep, despite the incredible shrieking of a caged bird in the apartment next to ours.

The next week, there was car trouble. There was an error that had been made on a project at work that required all of us to put in extra time and to accept equal blame. My husband and I bickered about who'd forgotten to put the credit card bill in the mail the month before. After the new bill came with the extraordinary late charge attached, we found the old bill, complete with a stamp, slipped down behind the dresser and the wall.

Throughout it all, I carried the pale green bungalow inside me. Its garden gate. The purple flowers in the slightly overgrown windowboxes. The sunlight in the living room. The little flushed girl in her mother's arms. The taste of the water in the glass. The sweet, empty tang of that.

When Saturday finally came, I headed back.

I would not, of course, bother the woman again. I would simply walk past. I would explore the neighborhood around and beyond the house. I would try not even to pause outside it—although I knew it would be next to impossible not to pause. But I didn't want to alarm the woman, or make her suspicious. If she saw me again, she would doubt the truth of what I'd told her the first time, that I had simply been a passerby, admiring.

This was another glorious summer day in the neighborhood. The few clouds in the sky looked like paintings of clouds. The grass was even greener. There were small, jewellike birds sitting on the telephone wires. Through open windows as I walked, I could smell coffee, bacon. I could hear children singing childish songs, and now and then a hammer pounding away at something in a backyard. The few people I passed on the sidewalks or saw sitting on their porches looked content. They nodded. They waved. If people were losing their houses, selling them in desperation for songs, they were hiding their troubles well. Everyone, it seemed, had a rocking chair, a calico cat, a flowering shrub under a picture window.

I turned right at Vervain Lane. My heart was fluttering—impractically—in my chest as I saw the little green bungalow up ahead.

Its gate. Its windowboxes.

But this time the gate wasn't latched. It was wide open. As I approached, I was half hoping and half dreading that the woman would be in the front yard, that she might be gardening or playing with her little girl, that she would recognize me and invite me in again. Another glass of that pure water. This time, she might be able to offer me a tour of the other rooms, which might have been tidied since I was last there.

But it wasn't her. There was a different woman in the front yard this morning. This woman's hair was short and gray. She wore a dark suit, carried a clipboard. She was walking unsteadily on what appeared to be high heels around on the grass, which had grown a great deal since the week before. Nearly a foot. It was halfway up the woman's shins. She seemed to be inspecting the windows from where she stood in the grass, or maybe she was looking up at the roof or the eaves, hand held to her forehead as a visor. She dropped the hand and turned around quickly when she heard my footsteps on the sidewalk behind her.

"Jesus," she said. "You scared me." And then, apologetically, taking a step toward me. "Sorry. Jumpy."

I stopped, and rubbed my eyes. The house looked different. The flowers in the windowboxes were dead. The flowers in the garden looked dried-out, too, and nearly dead. There was a yellow sticker affixed to the front door. The gray-haired woman looked from me to the sticker, and back. "Foreclosure," she said in what sounded like a falsely sentimental voice. "A terrible tragedy."

"They've moved?" I asked. "The people who lived here?"

The woman looked at me as if waiting to see if I would go on. When I didn't, she said, "They lost the house. In over their heads."

"Oh, dear," I said. "Oh my God. I was just here last week."

The woman shrugged. "Well, it's empty now." She pointed at the windowboxes and then waved her hands at the overgrown lawn, as if to prove her point. "Are you house-hunting? I'm not the realtor. I'm with the bank. But I'm fairly certain you could buy this place now for a song if you wanted. Have you spoken with the realtor?"

"No," I said. "I just admired it. The house. I met the woman who lived here, and her child. We can't afford a house at the moment anyway. Not yet. I just thought it was so—"

"When?" The woman eyed me suspiciously. Her lips were pursed. "When did you meet the Bells?"

"I didn't know their name was Bell," I said. "I never even asked her name. It was only one time. Last weekend. Last Saturday."

The gray-haired woman waded toward me, her heels catching in the soft ground and the long grass. She tucked the clipboard under her arm. She licked her lower lip, seemed to think for a moment before she said, "Then it wasn't the Bells. Do you know what happened to the Bells?"

"No," I said.

"Well, you didn't meet the Bells last weekend. After the foreclosure, they sold all their furniture and things. The house was completely empty, and they only had twenty-four hours to get out, but they never got themselves another place to live. They were sleeping on the floor, it seems, since they sold their things. When the bank came to change the locks, they wouldn't leave."

I held up a hand. This was none of my business. And it was also a lie. Or I was in the middle of some mistake. No point in hearing the erroneous details. I had the wrong house. The wrong time of day. It was no longer summer. A year had passed. Or two. I was simply confused. I'd read this in the news. Some sort of horror that occurred to desperate people. I'd had a bad dream. I would wake up from this dream. We were all having the same dream. Those of us without houses, and those of us with houses. Things were changing. It would take a while to get used to this new order of things. We saw their yellow stickers, of course, all over town, and their For Sale signs, but surely those people bought other houses after they left those houses, after we bought their houses for a song.

In other neighborhoods. Or other towns.

And so on, and so on.

Surely, their lives went on.

"It's quite a tragedy," the woman from the bank said. "I'm surprised you hadn't heard."

Had I heard?

I took the hand that had been resting on the gate, then, and covered my mouth. I had to keep my hand over my mouth for several minutes while the gray-haired woman watched me anxiously before I trusted myself to take the hand away, and to speak again without singing a song.

Search Continues for Elderly Man

There was a child on the porch, a boy. He had a dog on a leash. The boy and the dog looked up at me. The boy was smiling. The dog was panting as if it had been running. I said, "Yes?"

"Mr. Rentz?"

"Yes?" I said.

"Don't you remember us?" the boy asked.

Behind him, a tractor rumbled by on the gravel road. A cloud of dust rose behind the tractor. A young farmer in a white T-shirt took one hand off the wheel and waved. I lifted my hand to wave back, but the farmer had only glanced in my direction for a second, less than a second, before rumbling away.

"*What?*" I said, leaning down to the boy.

Of course, I'd heard what he'd said, my hearing was perfect, but I'd already forgotten what it was I'd heard. The dog—some kind of terrier—had begun to wag its tail, whining excitedly on its leash, as if it were anticipating something from me, as if it expected me to open the door.

"I just asked," the boy said, looking a bit amused, "if you remembered us."

"Oh," I said.

Behind the boy, on the other side of the gravel road, there was a young girl running bare-legged, leaping through the field. She had a handful of clover, or something blurred and purple, and she was shrieking. I watched her for a few moments, and then, as if she'd slipped into a hole in the earth, both she and her shrieks were gone.

I looked back down at the boy and his dog. *Yes,* I thought, there was certainly something familiar here. The boy's chipped front tooth. But also that dog.

"We were in the neighborhood," the boy said, "and we remembered your house, and wondered if you wanted to come out, if you could come out and play."

I snorted a little, of course. *Come out and play.* I supposed this was supposed to bring it all back—those childhood years, those carefree summer days! I supposed this boy was supposed to be some hallucinated version of me. I supposed that dog was supposed to be my dog, way back when, and here was Death at my door, beckoning me outside "to play," and I was supposed to step out there and follow the boy into the field, and maybe later he'd get me to take his hand, and we'd find ourselves back at my mother's table with a big ham at the center and all my dead relatives would be shiny-eyed and happy to see me, and in a startling epiphanic moment of ambivalence and ecstasy I'd suddenly understand that the boy, who was me, was dead. But I'd never had a dog.

And my mother had packed me up by the age of four and sent me to live with Aunt Elizabeth, who was an all-out drunk. The kind of drunk who'd manage to get dinner on the table every few nights, and then would stumble into the table and knock it all onto the floor, then chase me and that girl, Francine, and that other orphan, whose name I'm not sure I ever even knew, around with a broken bottle screaming that she was going to kill us all. When Uncle Ernest would get home, he'd sock her in the mouth, and we'd all go salvage whatever we could from the floor for supper. If there was ever a dog, it would have run off.

"I'm busy," I said to the boy, and the dog sat down then, as if on cue, on its haunches. The boy narrowed his eyes. Yes, there was certainly something sinister about the kid. Anyone could see that, even a confused old man. I knew right away that he wouldn't be taking no for an answer.

"That's too bad," the boy said. His voice was lower this time around. Overhead, a plane came barreling out of a cloud, crashing in only seconds somewhere over the horizon, never making a sound. He hooked a thumb in over his belt buckle as if he might yank his pants down. As if he were planning to take a piss or a shit right there on my stoop. The little dog curled his lip a bit, like he was thinking about growling.

"Now, look," I said. "I do know you. I know all about you, and you can stand out here on my stoop all day and do whatever foul thing you can think up to do, but I'm not coming out . . ." and then I added, sarcastically, "*to play,*" so he'd know I wasn't quite the sentimental old doddering fool he'd taken me for.

He frowned. And then he shrugged. He started to turn around. "Fine," he said. "Have it your way."

He headed back down the steps. The dog turned to follow him.

I couldn't help it. I'd been expecting trouble. All my life, there it had been, every time I opened the god-damned door. First Aunt Elizabeth, of course. And then the disastrous marriage. Anne with hands like claws within two years of the honeymoon, twisted up like a crabapple tree in the rollaway bed, the whole house smelling of death, and still a hundred chores dawn to dusk to be done. And the children. A limb now and then. A shovel brought down accidentally on some neighbor kid's head. "You just wait a minute you little bastard," I said.

He turned back around, slowly, and this time he had a whole new face. The face of an angel! His voice was as sweet as a girl's. The dog had cocked its head, sweetly. And then it vanished. Just a blank space on a limp leash. The angel said, "Yes, Mr. Rentz? *Yes?*"

It was hard not to give right in. But I knew what this was about. I hadn't avoided this encounter for eighty years just to walk straight into its booby trap now. I hadn't forgotten the way Duke and Erma had signed over that insurance policy to their son just before the thing in the ravine. Duke with his foot in a coyote trap and a plastic bag over his face. Erma . . . and them making it look like a rape, but nobody would have raped poor crippled Erma. The devil, maybe.

No. Not even the devil.

I took a step backward. I raised up both fists. I said, "I know you know I can fight. I know you've fought me before. And you remember what happened then."

"Oh, Mr. Rentz." He said it as if he were tired of this particular fight. *Yes, yes, yes.* Those nurses with their pockets full of pills. Those prostitutes down on Division Avenue, tapping on the window of your car. I'd fallen for this once or twice, but whoever that poor fellow was, I was not him anymore. The farmer on the tractor came chugging by again, but he came from the same direction he'd come from the last time. They couldn't even get this part right. They were just running the same film twice. Trying to save money, I supposed, thinking an old man wouldn't notice. This time, when he waved, I didn't bother to raise my hand.

The boy seemed to be trying to stifle a laugh.

I'd always had a bad temper.

Of course, it made me mad.

And then the girl again. The clover, the bare legs, the hole. I was shaking. It was like that copy of the copy of the copy of the letter my mother had written to me, dug up out of the trunk by my daughter, which she'd mailed off to everybody and their cousin before she thought to bring it over to me. *Daddy, I found this in the attic, and I thought you'd want a copy.*

And my own mother's handwriting, like a retarded child's.

And she couldn't even spell the name of the month.

Which was February.

And something about when I get you back I'm going to get you that little dog.

That little dog.

It was back. But it was behind me. It was smiling up at me from my own rug. And then it was on the couch. And then it was under the coffee table. Pissing on the leg of it. Taking a crap on the carpet.

Then lunging in my direction. Then snapping at me heels. Then tearing at the cuffs of my trousers with its teeth. *Get outta here, get outta here.* I was kicking at it, and the girl was screaming, *Help help, someone get him offa me.* But I didn't care about that. I was going to have her if it was the last thing I ever had. My pants were down around my ankles, and I was sure as hell going to stick it inside her, and then some fat woman in white stepped out into the waiting room and said, only her eyebrow twitching a little, *I'm sorry to tell ya the baby has died.* I shrugged. I said, *D'ya tell my wife?*

Soon enough, I'd stumbled out the door, just as I'm sure they'd planned it. The dog sobered up and started whining to be petted. The little boy said, "I *knew* you'd come out to play, Mr. Rentz. I knew it! I knew it!" The tractor and the farmer and the little girl, as if someone up there just kept hitting *rewind rewind.* That girl stood up and I could see my seed trickling down her thigh. I stifled a laugh, chuckling behind my hand, *How stupid do you think I am?*

Well, that's how stupid I am.

And then I heard the door slam behind me.

And then the boy turned to look at me with those big serious eyes and said, "I'm sorry to have had to mislead you, Mr. Rentz."

And I said, "Oh, kid, forget it. I understand." And then we shuffled off into the dust, the two of us—the beautiful boy I might have been and the dog I might have had—in search of the old lost man I had become.

The Barge

One Wednesday a barge got stuck beneath the bridge. We were children, and we loved this fateful accident, this trouble occurring to others, this summer entertainment conducted under a bridge, just for us. We stood on the bridge all day looking down, waving our little stripes and stars at their hammers and sickles.

The men on the barge were patient with us. They had children of their own. They'd been stuck many times on barges under bridges in their own country in the past—which was a gray woolen blanket behind them, sodden with memories, like the sea.

They smoked cigarettes, ran their hands over the tops of their heads, waited for something to happen.

Rag-Anne was with me on Wednesday on the bridge.

Rag-Anne had been with me since the beginning.

I'd woken up in this world behind bars in a crib with Rag-Anne beside me—back when she was new and all her stitches were pulled tight and her yarn hair was blond and I wore a ribbon and called my father Daddy. She was as real to me as the friends around me on the bridge that day—with their dirty faces, eating candy they wouldn't let me taste on sticks—but she was a doll. Gray and limp and made of thinning cloth. I'd long since swallowed her button eyes. There were grease spots on her apron.

But, of course, I was also growing older. I had dirt on my knees that no amount of scrubbing could wash off. One day when I crawled into my father's lap and called him Daddy, he pushed me off.

"Ugh, does that thing have to sit at the table with us?" my father would ask, looking at Rag-Anne looking at him from her seat at the end of the table.

"Oh, just a little longer," my mother said in the small voice she only used when he was in the room. "Someone's birthday's coming up!"

Oh, the birthday, the *birthdaycomingup*. There was a doll I'd seen at the department store and wanted and been assured I would have. That doll's human hair reflected the department store light, and her eyes were made of human glass and her skin of human plastic, like all the dolls at the department store I'd always wanted and had yet to have.

But the doll on the bridge above the barge with me that day was named for my grandmother Anne, who'd died alone in a back room of our house two winters before, unraveling like a sweater or a shadow in her bed as I played with the doll by the fire and turned up the volume on the television so I couldn't hear the other Anne struggle for breath on the other side of the wall.

Anne, and Anne.

On and on.

But everything came to an end in the end.

"Your doll's never been on a barge," my friend Rachel's older brother said in a false baby voice. "She wants to give it a try."

Once, this boy had snatched a piece of watermelon out of my hand and eaten it in front of me while I screamed. Once, he'd grabbed the tail feathers of a dead bird in a ditch, and flung it at me. Once, he'd stuck a handful of snow down the front of my pants— keeping the hand there as the snow melted, staring into my eyes as if he were seeing into my brain.

That bird he'd flung managed to fly, flapping its wings mechanically over my head for a few seconds before it fell in front of me in a soggy heap to die a second time, and the soggy heap of that bird was what he saw inside my brain.

And the snow—I told my mother about the snow, and she put her dishtowel to the side of her head and said, "Oh dear, oh dear, don't say another word about it. You don't want Daddy to find out."

I expected Rachel's older brother to grab the doll from my hands and toss her over the bridge. I realized in that moment that I had been prepared since the day I was born for this boy to grab my doll and throw her over a bridge. I wouldn't even gasp, I knew, when he did it. I would let him. I would watch.

But he didn't.

He just looked at Rag-Anne, at me, and then down at the men on the barge. They were patient down there, but they were also tired. This was no longer a game to them. The air was maritime gray. Rag-Anne looked at me with no eyes. *Please*, she said, speaking to me with no eyes. *Please?*

She meant the bridge, the barge, the men below us. Please.

What?

Please, you know what.

Please.

She was trying to explain to me what I already knew but had not entirely believed. That she was getting older, as was I. That everything was about to change—whether we accepted the change, whether we set it in motion ourselves, or tried to prevent it, or not. That there was *birthdaycomingup*. That there would be a new doll with blond hair and human eyes, and what would become of Rag-Anne then.

We knew. We knew. We knew.

Why not?

Why not, while there was still this chance. While there was still this barge below us on this bridge. Who knew how long until this chance, this barge, was gone forever from our lives. Could she not just, perhaps, please, give this other life a try?

No, I thought, clinging to her more tightly.

Rachel's older brother smirked. The others watched.

No.

No eyes.

When he touched her with a finger, she didn't even flinch. His smirk, his dirty finger. It seemed she didn't even mind.

"Just let her try," he said, almost kindly.

Please, she said. Oh, please. How long anyway is any doll's life? How long, anyway could any life go on. My grandmother had finally been taken from our house on a stretcher borne aloft by a muscular woman and a small man. They'd burned her up. I knew that much. I saw the urn, and overheard.

"Toss her over," my friend's brother said. "Go on."

He didn't need to speak to me like a baby now. Now, I understood the language we were speaking. *Toss me over, Please.* It was what she would have said with eyes if she still had eyes, if her eyes were not lodged deep inside me. I looked at her, at him, and then—

Then she slipped, feathered death, over the railing of the bridge, sighing into the oncoming twilight below us, and my friend's older brother poked me gently between my legs with his finger—a burning branch unfurling itself all through my body and sprouting out of the back of my skull when he did—while the other children laughed, and he said, "Good job, idiot."

For whom did I cry all the way home and into the bathtub that night?

Rag-Anne?

No.

I'd cast her off on purpose. I'd hated her, and her decay, her frayed gray petticoat, her grease-stained apron, even her name.

Rag-Anne, and also Anne.

I'd hated them both—but especially my grandmother, who'd burned a hole in me by dying, by allowing herself to be burned alive. I could stick three fingers into that hole, wiggle them around— bloodless, painless, but also terrible. I'd wanted those two out of my sight.

And, yet, I felt afraid. The men on the barge seemed not to have noticed that a doll had fallen into their midst. Who knew what they might do when they did. They might cast her into the water. They might set her on fire.

That night, an enormous hairless zoo animal made of silence slipped into my dream, lay down on top of me, and stayed there, like a warm snow pile, until morning. Then, we all went back to the bridge and saw her: Anne!

I knew it was her by the expression on her face. I had been looking at that face for years, and it had never changed, even without eyes.

The boys whistled, but not loud enough for the men smoking on the barge to hear. The men on the barge were watching her, paying no attention to the children overhead.

She was blond now, again, in a thin fresh flowered dress. No underwear, it seemed. I could see a black triangle between her legs, the button eyes of her nipples. There was a smear of fiery lipstick on her mouth. Where had she gotten it? Even my grandmother had never worn lipstick.

She was laughing as she sat on their laps. One man's lap, and then another's. She was barefoot, black-eyed, very young. When one of the men on the barge pointed a cigarette in our direction, she looked up, holding a hand to her forehead.

Was she saluting, or blocking the sun?

She waved at us with her other hand, and we waved our little American flags back at her, and the boys stuck out their tongues. The men on the barge grabbed at her small breasts, and she just laughed and let them—and then she was gone, and then she was gone, down in the bowels of the barge.

Anne, my grandmother, my rag doll animated by their new world down there below the bridge, on the barge, their wild new life, which was entirely my fault, my hideous idea entirely, my brave idea that had saved them from the fire.

You know the rest.

The bridge. The barge. A church bell clapping in the distance along with the echoing sneeze of a metal tool banging on a metal roof—as if it were a competition between heaven and earth, as if heaven had the slightest hope of winning.

It was hot down there, and they took turns, and they came back out into the sun, pulling on their shirts, zipping up their pants, one by one, one by one, until each of them was done, and then the barge began to pull away, and all of it was gone.

And all of it was gone.

And I started to cry again, and he touched me with his finger between my legs again, almost tenderly, my friend's older brother, and he said, "Shut up, you idiot."

It was Thursday. Nothing like that ever happened again.

You're Going to Die

Their father had "only a short time," as the doctors put it, and it had fallen to the eldest daughter to tell him this. "He would want to know," the other three of his children said with certainty, "and he'd want to hear it from you," and then they went back to their lives.

She would take him out in the boat, she thought, on the river. She would row. He could lean back and watch the sky, watch the clouds slip around in it like afterthoughts—never the same cloud twice. Soft craters. Calm bombs. Floating. Dispersing. Reanimating and reforming. Surely, this was the place to do it. Here the news would seem less personal. Cosmic news. A part of the cycle of this life, there in the boat with his eldest daughter, his hand in hers. You are going to die, she would say, and he would nod, staring up into the blue inevitability of the sky.

But that morning when she picked him up he looked fantastic. His hair was combed, and there was color in his cheeks. He was wearing a cap and a tweed jacket like some father out of a Russian fairy tale, not like her father. She found herself peering around him, as if for the ragged old man she'd expected, and glimpsed the little foreign nurse's aide slipping out of his room like a ripple, or a giggle, wearing white. The aide's name was something decorated with accent marks and vowels that made the opposite of the sound they ordinarily made, as if the name had been conceived as a way to shame her own, plain name. Jane. When that aide had to speak to Jane, she called her "Mrs.," although Jane had never married.

Jane's father had a handkerchief folded into an arrowhead in his pocket this morning. Had the aide done this for him? It was embroidered with initials Jane didn't recognize—not his own initials. His pants looked pressed. Perhaps he'd put on a bit of weight. He called good-bye to his aide, who called back to him in a language Jane didn't speak, and her father didn't speak, but which he seemed to understand.

You are going to die.

"Daddy," Jane said. "You're going to be too hot in that jacket. You should leave it in the car."

He looked at her blankly, and then he shrugged, as if he were the tracks shrugging off the train, as if he were the hero of a tale shrugging off his fate. He kept the jacket.

Jane started the car and drove in the direction of the canoe livery, listening to her car's little alarm bell chime the whole way because her father wouldn't buckle his seat belt. She'd considered sitting in the parking lot of the retirement home with him until he agreed to let her fasten it, but then she reminded herself that he was going to die. What did it matter, and how much longer would she need to listen to that bell chiming as she drove her stubborn father places anyway? When she started the car without starting the old argument, she was quite sure she saw, in the passenger window, the reflection of his smile. He'd won an argument without even having to have it, an art he'd perfected in the course of his life.

When they came to a stop at a red light, Jane turned to look at him, seatbelt warning chiming between them, seatbelt light flashing on the dashboard in front of her, and he was definitely smiling, and he was wearing that jacket and looking like a man in perfect health, as pleased with himself as ever, the same guy who'd greeted her every morning when she was a teenager by crowing, "Hey there. Somebody took her ugly pills again this morning!" The same guy who'd unwrapped every Christmas present she'd ever agonized over before buying and set it down on the floor at his feet never to speak of it again.

"What's your problem?" he asked her.

In the corner of her eye Jane saw that the traffic light had turned green, but there were no other drivers around, and they were certainly in no hurry. She made no effort to step on the gas and pass through the intersection.

"Huh. What's with you. Forget how to drive? Waiting for the light to turn a little greener. Take too many stupid pills this morning?"

Jane didn't swallow. She didn't even take a deep breath. She said, "You're going to die."

The Flowering Staff

It was a homely little trailer, but it was strung with plastic pink flamingo lights that blinked electrically as Zak and Angela pulled up, and there was a bush next to a little cement patio—waxy dark-green leaves and blossoms the color of the flamingos. Its petals had fallen around it in several layers, as if the bush had been generating and discarding its own beauty for years without interference in that very spot.

Two folding chairs sat with a TV tray between them. A yellow canopy stretched over it all. This looked like a nice place. Angela unrolled her window, and Zak could smell the sweet decay beyond their rental car. Sun-lush foliage. Overripe fruit. A kind of moisturizer his grandmother used on the cracked skin of her feet, the flaking skin of her shins, the inflamed skin of her knees.

But it was a good smell. Fragrant. Mixed up now with what must have been the air rising over the deep slow-creeping waters of the canal he'd seen as they pulled into the Linger Longer Village.

They had come to Florida so he could meet Angela's mother, who was an old woman, older than Zak's oldest grandmother, before he and Angela married. Angela herself was fourteen years older than Zak ("Old enough to be your mother!" his own mother had cried out when he told her) although no one would guess this. At forty,

Angela looked younger than most of the girls his friends were dating. Unless he told them how old she was (and now he wished he never had) they assumed she was his age. Maybe a year or two older because she drove such an expensive car.

Even in a bikini. Even in harsh light.

Until he'd told them her age and then they'd learned that she'd been his professor, that she had two children from her first marriage, none of his friends had said anything but *Whoa, Dude.*

("Robbing the coffin!" his brother, that asshole, had chortled.)

"I should probably drive," Angela said after they threw their suitcases into the trunk at the airport. "These Florida drivers are insane. You'll see."

Zak was happy not to drive. He'd never been to Florida. He could look around while Angela drove.

But there had been some stress on the freeway, and now that they were parked in front of her mother's trailer Zak could see that Angela's knuckles were still white. From the airport to the Linger Longer Village, she'd driven without speaking, leaning into the steering wheel, and Zak had known better than to try to talk to her. He'd looked out the window instead: An astounding amount of sunlight. Unrecognizable flora and fauna. Green tangled around green. Brilliantly shining vehicles passed them at alarmingly high speeds, many of them driven by white-haired men or women seeming dwarfed by the chrome around them, appearing to be in the clutches of their own terrible creations. The freeway itself seemed made of velvet—soft and black and running ahead of them in an endless bolt. As Angela was easing the rental car through three lanes of sparking hubcaps and antennas and door handles, Zak had the feeling that they were traveling across some barrier made out of the exploded bits and pieces of space shuttles, that they were dodging the jagged diamonds between time zones. Everything was really weirdly bright and new.

Then, just past the entrance to the Linger Longer Village, Angela had grown confused, glancing furtively around her at the trailers lining the narrow, winding drive. She hadn't been to visit her mother in six years because her research and her two children from her first marriage had kept her too busy to fly to Florida except in emergencies. There'd been no emergencies.

"I can't remember which one is my mother's," Angela said, mostly to herself, and kept driving—slowly but steadily, deeper into the park, which was dense with palm trees and viney plants and some kind of dripping moss. Somehow the sun was managing to shine through the vegetation, but it cast gnarled shadows. Then, they passed a canal. Branches and dead leaves and what looked like a flotilla of sodden spinach traveled down the frothed brown water.

Angela slowed down then to try to puzzle out the trailers, and which one might be her mother's when, out of the shadows, an old man began to hobble toward them. This old man was headed straight toward them down the center of the road, and was leaning on a cane decorated with white (plastic?) flowers. He wore a plaid shirt. His bony legs were exposed beneath his white Bermuda shorts. Those legs looked alarmingly like chicken wings, except for the bulbous knees. Angela stopped the car and stared straight at him, making quiet snorting noises through her nose, as if readying herself for some kind of confrontation—but the old man just continued in their direction until he was only a few feet from their bumper, and then he veered around them, without looking at them, continuing to walk and continuing to lean on his flowered cane.

"Jesus Christ," Angela said.

Now, they were parked outside the trailer that must have been her mother's, but Angela made no movements that indicated that she planned to get out of the car, so Zak sat beside her, waiting.

There was no breeze, it seemed, but that bush with the pink flowers seemed to shiver beside the patio as if there were. From a palm tree that seemed to disappear in the sky overhead, there was the sudden raucous cawing of what sounded like several different kinds of birds competing in different languages. It was, Zak thought, what it might sound like if you stuck your head in a birdcage at the zoo.

"You're not going to *marry* her?" his mother had said. Her mouth had stayed open, and Zak could see her back teeth. They looked like a damp mountain range. He could suddenly imagine his mother dead, lying on her back in a coffin. He would miss her. It would just be him and his worthless brother after that. Except for Angela. Her two kids. He and his mother stood facing one another in the kitchen. Outside he could hear his brother whacking at golf balls in the grass, but he must have been missing them. It sounded as if he were whacking the heads off the tulips, or swinging at the seedy wigs of dandelions.

"Yeah, Mom. I am. We're getting married."

He'd tried not to sound apologetic or defensive. He truly understood his mother's concerns. But he supposed he sounded hypnotized, maybe, or under some other kind of duress. His mother had closed her mouth then, and turned her back. He thought he heard her mutter, "You'll be sorry," but he couldn't be sure. It was not the kind of thing his mother would say. She might have said, "That'll be lovely." She might have said nothing. She might have spoken a few words from the New Testament.

Zak and Angela went to pick out her wedding dress a few days later, and that night Zak had dreamed he was in a gym full of brides. Cake, lace, foamy whiteness. They were all young, and Zak knew he could have his pick, but mostly he just wanted to play basketball. He could see the balls in the corner. He could smell the solid rubber of them. Where were the baskets? There were no baskets.

The door of the trailer flew open, and a woman tumbled out, and the door slammed behind her with a startling clap. Zak sat up straighter in the passenger seat. He thought he heard Angela gasp. The woman yanked open the driver's side door, stuck her torso in. From where he sat Zak could only see the top of her head. White curls, pink scalp. But then he made out the trembling flesh of her upper arms. ("Take a good look," Greg had said. "Your mother-in-law's what your girlfriend will look like when she's fifty. . . . Oh, wait, your girlfriend's already fifty!" Ha. Ha.)

Angela was led from the car. She looked weak with exhaustion, Zak thought, although she'd fallen deeply asleep on his shoulder during the flight to Florida. Planes put her to sleep. They'd flown together to Rome when they were secretly in love, when he was still her student, and she'd slept then, too—completely and alarmingly for the entire duration of the flight over the Atlantic as his arm went numb beneath her and he stared into the burning lamp over his seat, wishing he could also sleep.

Now, she appeared as if a spell had been cast on her, as if she'd taken a shot of novocaine straight to the brain. Her pale blue skirt was creased, and her white tank top looked damp with sweat. Her tennis-toned arm was outstretched before her as her mother guided her toward one of the lawn chairs, and settled her into it, and then turned to the car, gesturing to Zak with wide wobbling sweeps of her own pale arm.

Joy radiated off the old woman like the light off a pile of diamonds. He had never seen anyone who looked happier in his life, not even actresses who'd been paid millions of dollars in movies to look happy.

Zak was directed to the lawn chair beside Angela's with the TV tray between them, and beers and cookies were fetched from the trailer. He kept glancing over at Angela, but she did not look back. They were like the king and queen of the place, in lawn chair thrones, looking out upon their subjects as the neighbors began to hobble by.

"My son and daughter!" Angela's mother announced.

Some of the onlookers had silver walkers. Many had canes. One came by in a motorized wheelchair. A few managed to snail past without aid. It was a slow-motion parade, and Zak tried several times to stand, to offer his chair to—

"Sit!" Angela's mother said, pressing him back down.

The man with the flowered cane came by, again down the center of the lane. This time he had his hand poked through the white handles of a Winn-Dixie bag. He bowed before Zak, holding out the bag. Zak took it and looked inside. A fat red tomato, an enormous peach, and what appeared to Zak to be some new kind of fruit—bright yellow, rugged, spiked.

"Thank you," Zak said.

He looked over at Angela again, holding the bag open for her so she could see inside, but she seemed too dazed to register the gift even as she gazed upon it. She glanced from the bag to Zak, and then back to the bag and the alien fruits within, and Zak could see that she was suffering in some way, but what could he do? Her eyes were pale blue. They were the first things he'd noticed about her when she'd clipped into the classroom three years earlier and announced that she was Professor Butler, but that they could call her Angela. And then her ass, which had been tucked neatly into a black suede skirt, when she turned to the blackboard.

Now, she was a ghost wearing those assets. A stranger in familiar clothes.

The old man nodded to Zak, and turned, heading slowly in the direction from which he'd come bearing that dead branch that had miraculously bloomed.

"My son and daughter!" Angela's mother continued to shout to all who gathered to look at them. "My angel and her betrothed. My beautiful daughter and the prince whose heart she has captured. *Look* at them. *Behold!*"

"Eh?!" an old lady called, cupping a hand around her ear. The old woman looked like a bird. She was so thin that nothing was left of her face but her beak and her teeth and her wrinkled lips. "Eh?" she cried out again, searching with her deaf ear for some explanation. *Eh?* a bird overhead answered her with a perfect imitation of her, but no one else bothered to explain anything to the old woman, and when Zak opened his mouth to try to introduce himself, Angela reached over with a hand so cold and damp it seemed she'd been soaking it in rainwater for days. She clamped her fingers around his wrist and applied a kind of trembling pressure that caused Zak to sink deeply into his lawn chair—so deeply he couldn't possibly have escaped the old woman approaching him now, reaching out to take his face in her spotted hands, bringing her own face down to his for what he suspected would be a long and lingering kiss.

The Prisoners

A girl woke up, and it was summer. There were handfuls of soft hair on her head, which rested on a pillow that seemed to be filled with feathers. She sat up slowly, blinking, looking around, aware that at one time she might have known this place she found herself in, this season outside the window beside her, but no longer.

Better get out of bed, she thought. She might be late for something. She recalled that being late had always been frowned upon—by someone, for some reason. She placed her feet on the floor: Feet. Floor.

She looked out the window.

Apparently she'd slept for a very long time because she certainly had no recollection of a forest. How long did it take for so many trees to grow so tall?

No.

She did not remember any forest at all. Something else had been outside the window. Something flat. And blue. Sky? No. What had they called it. Puddle. Pond. *Pool.*

Pool.

But it had not been summer then, for swimming. It had been winter, and the pool had been empty of water. Drained. It had only been painted blue. But snow fell into it, and onto the bodies of the Prisoners.

How had she known they belonged to the Prisoners, those bodies? Ribbons? Ripples? Stripples? *Stripes.*

She had recognized their uniforms by their gray and white stripes. Names.

They'd had them. But not simple names, like Matt, like Ben. (Her brothers!) But not just numbers either, like the Patients.

What had she called her favorite Prisoner?

Rotor? Roper? Rotund? *Fatty!*

Fatty had been only skin and bones. He'd had yellowish eyes, and had made her laugh. She'd fed him—what? Little pills. Bread crumbs. Lozenges. Pinches of sugar, butter, something?

Dinner mints!

He'd catch them on his tongue and do a little dance on his artificial leg.

"Stay away from the Prisoners!" the tall pale lady would scream, running across the green, holding her skirts up to her knees.

But she would not stay away from Fatty, whom she'd loved. And also the other one. Witness. His name had been Witness! She did not need to think any harder to remember *him.* His eyes had been pecked out by birds, so they had called him Witness. How could she ever forget? He'd almost scared her to death the first time he'd asked to touch her hand with his own, but his own hand had been surprisingly cool and soft—and those blank holes in his face where he'd once had eyes, when she'd gotten used to them, she could have stared into those smooth sockets all day if they'd let her. *Everything* was in them. The wagons, the gypsies, the campfires blazing despite the rain, the whole history of the Kingdom. The tundra her ancestors had crossed to reach it. Their bark boats in the middle of an ocean with great chunks of ice floating in it. And the men in their reindeer skins, and the women dressed as birds—ten thousand feathers fluttering around their heads.

Now she remembered. She'd watched them hang Witness one afternoon, and then cut him down still twitching, thrown his body onto the others at the bottom of the drained swimming pool. His eyes had been open. He'd been looking straight at her. And then—

And then nothing. No one. For so long.

How long?

How long did it take for a forest to grow?

She put her hand to the windowpane. It was cold. In the air out there, a bit of snow. What did they call this season again?

Witness?

No, winter.

And wasn't that also her own name, and the name of her kingdom, and the name of her country, and—?

No. No. Something else was on the tip of her tongue. What could it have been?

Whither, wisdom, whisper, whimper, whistler?

Swimmer, glister, jester, luster, laughter?

She was on her knees with her face in her hands when she heard footsteps climbing stairs.

Psalter, ranter, rooster, banish, answer?

And then she heard the jangling of keys. The clearing of a throat. Static crackling over some kind of radio. Bitter laughter.

I Hope This Is Hell

The check-out line snakes clear down aisle thirteen to the paper towel display, and then up past the plastic utensils and packaged napkins. Everyone seems to be buying their Fourth of July picnic supplies late. It *is* the Fourth of July. Like these others, Chloe has no choice but to stand in the line. The things in her cart, she has to buy. There will be company. It's the Fourth of July. Last week, her husband, driving to work in his pickup truck, struck a child on a bicycle, and two days ago the child died.

It was only a mile from their own front door, at the bottom of the hill, at an intersection through which they'd passed without incident every day, thousands of times, for years. It was a two-lane road, paved, but in the country. A yellow line ran straight down the middle of it, broken here and there to let the faster vehicles pass the old people and the tractors. There was a stop sign at the end of it. There was a house up on the hill where a nurse lived—a nurse who had already left for her own job by the time Chloe's husband came running up the driveway, the bloody boy in his arms, calling for help.

He'd set the child down in an old lawn chair and broken down the nurse's front door to get in, to call 911.

There is an angry man in front of her in the line.

"This place," he says, shaking his head. "Jesus Christ."

She nods. The man is cradling four enormous bags of potato chips in his arms. They look difficult to hold. So airy, so insubstantial. But awkward, too. A delicate balance. If you held on too tightly, they would crumble into potato ashes. If you let go, who knows.

"What's the matter with this place?" he asks Chloe, really *looking* at her, as if she might actually have an answer.

She shrugs. She offers, weakly, "Not enough help?"

The man snorts and looks away. Chloe has given him the wrong answer. He wanted to hear something damning. Something inherent. Something premeditated. He wanted to blame someone *specific*. An older woman in front of the man turns to look at Chloe then as if either criticizing her for being critical, or also waiting for a better answer. The woman's hair in the bright grocery store appears so thin that Chloe could count the brown spots on her scalp without taking even one step closer. A cartoonish image flashes in front of her of sneezing in the old woman's direction, and the hair being blown right off her head in a wispy explosion while the old woman, with big, surprised eyes, grabs her naked scalp, feeling around for the hair.

The woman stares at Chloe awhile longer, and then says, as if she, too, had been asked for her opinion, "I don't know. The whole franchise is bad."

This, Chloe knows for a fact to be true. When she lived in Pascua, she shopped at its mother-store, and the lines there were even longer, the produce even paler, softer. As at this location, the fruit in the mother-store was always hovered over by a veil of fruit flies. Small moths occasionally wafted down the cereal aisle. Chloe suspected those moths were leaving larvae behind in the Frosted Flakes. Once, at the Pascua store, Chloe had dropped a grapefruit she'd meant to put in a plastic bag. When it hit the linoleum, instead of rolling, it had collapsed at her feet—deflated, putrid. A small crowd of housewives and elderly men had gathered to scoff at it. Disbelieving. Appalled. One old man had suggested that Chloe try to get her money back.

But Chloe hadn't paid for anything. What would she get her money back for?

Still, it *had* seemed like an injustice, a betrayal, the kind of thing for which a customer should be compensated. The way that grape-fruit had shone slickly under the fluorescent lights, and had been, in truth, full of rot, had seemed like a promise that had been broken.

Maybe it was even *more* of an injustice *because* she hadn't paid for anything, *because* this had just happened to her, and no one owed her a cent, not even a perfunctory apology.

It's a small town, and Chloe has lived in it for eight years. She's seen this man, the man in the line ahead of her, around the town on many occasions. Like her, he has a grown child, maybe a few years older than Chloe's daughter. Chloe has a fairly clear memory of seeing this man standing in the hallway of the high school with his arms crossed, glaring into the face of a boy who looked exactly like him.

But that must have been at least seven years ago, when Chloe still felt like an outsider in the town, when her daughter cried her-self to sleep every night because she missed her friends, her father, her old life, her old school. That was back when Chloe still woke up every morning so overwhelmed with guilt that she felt as if the pores of her skin might have released it all over her pillow as she slept.

She changed the sheets every other day.

Her new husband thought this was lovely, this changing of the sheets—evidence of Chloe's superiority to his first wife. He did a lot of comparison.

You're so much quieter than Danielle was. You're so much more orga-nized, so much more understanding. Your food is so much more colorful. You're so much better with money.

It was so consistent, so constant, that Chloe started to read between the lines.

He never told her, for instance, that she was better in bed than Danielle had been. He never told her that she was more beautiful. He never said that Chloe was funnier, or a better conversationalist, or more exciting. He'd pat her hip in bed before she fell into a deep sleep and say something cheery like, "I can't believe how lucky I am. You're so much more suited to me than Danielle. We're so much more alike."

It drove Chloe insane to think of Jay feeling about her the way she'd felt about her ex-husband—*here's my pal, my companion, my doppelgänger, the opposite-sex equivalent of* me—when what she felt for Jay was outrageous curiosity, nearly scandalous intrigue, regarding every aspect of who he was.

Chloe would lie awake in bed and think to herself, who wanted a wife who was that much *like* you?

So suited.

Suits, in fact, were one of the things her new husband liked to rail against. Men who had to wear them. Those sorry bastards. *Imagine* having to tie a noose around your neck every day before you left the house.

For her part, the reason Chloe had fallen in love with *him*, leaving behind her first husband and her first life, was because he was such a mystery to her. The barn full of implements. The pickup truck. The venison in the freezer. Before she canceled her subscription, a copy of the *Atlantic Monthly* was forwarded to her at her new husband's. He'd picked it up, and turned it over and over in his hands. "What the hell is this?" he'd asked, as if he'd never seen a magazine before, let alone the *Atlantic*. It set her pulse to racing, thinking of her first husband all weekend on a couch with the *Atlantic* in front of his face, his glasses pushed down on his nose so he could read without them. She might have pulled Jay into bed right then.

So many things about Jay, like this puzzlement at the *Atlantic Monthly*, made Chloe feel knocked over with relief and lust that sometimes it felt like the heavy, dumb, clobbering paws of a big dog against her chest. He was a stranger to her. He was utterly unsuited. Her friends thought she was nuts. Her daughter, during the bad period of her first adjustment to the divorce and the new life, had screamed, "He's a fucking *redneck*!"

"Gosh," her ex-husband had said when he'd picked their daughter up one weekend and met Jay for the first time, "are you planning to teach him to read?" Chloe was a reading teacher. After her ex-husband had left with her daughter, Chloe had nearly swooned with it. The laughter and delight. The honest lust. Jay had come out on the porch and looked at her as if he were completely confused, but happy enough. She'd thrown her arms around him. She'd demanded that, right that second, they go up to the bedroom and fuck.

These feelings, on her dark days, were the feelings she imagined he'd had for Danielle, who'd left him without a nickel. Jay was done, Chloe supposed, with that kind of love. Ready for something simpler: Chloe. Sometimes she still found Danielle's long black hairs in the dust mop. Sometimes, it took ten or eleven shakes out the back door to get those strands out of her dust mop, or off of her fingers.

But the years passed. Even her ex-husband was no longer angry. A few months before, her ex-husband had actually passed Chloe and Jay, in Jay's pickup, in his Saab, on the freeway, and Randall had set to honking and waving, a big smile on his face, as if he were astonished to find his two best friends driving beside him on the freeway. What a coincidence! At first, Chloe didn't even recognize him (new Saab, different color), but then his features assembled themselves one by one into a familiar face. Chloe knew this man well. He wasn't pretending to be happy to see them, he *was*.

And by now her daughter had quit with the bingeing and the purging and had finished a degree in creative writing from the university, with high honors and a slew of poetry awards, and had moved to San Francisco. Every few weeks she called home with some new exciting bit of information. An apartment overlooking the park! A date with a nice guy! A party at the office! A little promotion!

As the years passed, and the radical unforgivable decisions Chloe had made seemed less and less radical, more and more forgivable, Chloe had finally also come to terms with the fact that her husband could love her without being electrified by her, even if she were still, eight years later, still electrified by him. It was enough, wasn't it, to be loved so sincerely by someone? It was enough, wasn't it, to be the best cook someone had ever known, to keep the tidiest house, to be so much fun to go to a movie with? "You're my best friend," Jay had said more than once, seeming astonished at his good luck.

Still, it had only been, it seemed to Chloe, about a *week* since she'd grown used to this—all of this, her whole life, her strange decisions, like the decisions of a stranger—and accepted it, herself, and what she'd done.

Was that *possible*, to feel the passage of time so differently than the clocks and calendars registered it—or was that, as she suspected, some sort of distortion, like the little warning stenciled onto the bottom of the rearview mirror? Looking backward, she only *thought* that what she was seeing was the way things back there actually looked. Those things were smaller, distorted by hindsight, forever lost to actual understanding and analysis. Certainly, surely, Chloe could not honestly have named the date, pin-pointed the very moment, of her acceptance of *everything* after eight years of vicissitude and guilt?

No.

Yes.

Truly.

It *was* true. Chloe had recognized it even as it was happening: She was standing in the kitchen, pouring coffee into a cup, and Jay was pulling the front door closed behind him, brightly and casually telling her to have a good day.

"Be careful driving!" she'd called out to him.

It would have been less than a hundred and twenty seconds later that he was scooping the bloodied child up in his arms, running.

"I hope this is hell," the man in line ahead of her says, "because if there's something worse waiting for me, I don't think I can stand it."

Chloe would have pretended to chuckle if she could. She knows there's no point in the rage she feels, the impulse to tell the man in front of her in the check-out line what *hell* might really feel like, that *hell* might be a party in your backyard the week after your husband in his pickup truck has struck a child on a bicycle, two days after that child has been taken off life support—a party you'd thrown every year for the last seven years and which everyone insisted you should throw again this year, for your husband's sake, and which you'd foolishly, until this very moment, believed they were right about. A party for which guests would begin to arrive in about an hour, and you hadn't even wiped off the picnic table yet or set out the lawn chairs.

This man. In addition to that one time in the high school hallway, Chloe thinks she might remember having seen him once or twice at the post office. (He'd been grumbling there, too. But everyone had. A line clear out the door that time.) There's something about his face that makes Chloe think of Jesus, if he'd gotten to be about fifty years old. The eyes are dark and full of suffering, but he also looks too intelligent to put up with too much more bullshit from this world, unlike Christ. He needs a shave. He is, she realizes, a very attractive man.

She looks into her cart:

She's got the beer, the crackers, the Cracker Barrel cheese spread. The salami and rye bread. The chips and pretzels. The French onion dip.

But there were other things she should have gotten, should have prepared. Things she put out every year. Things her guests might have grown to expect. The meatballs. The fruit salad. But Chloe has neither the time, now, nor the heart to cut radishes into flowerets. Surely, they'd understand. The guests who hadn't already heard the news would find out fast from the whisperings behind the garage, and from the zombie-mask on her husband's face—a gray, damp-plaster thing he went to bed with every night now, woke up with, wore all day.

"Fuck. Fuck!" Jay had shouted after he hung up the phone.

He was standing at the edge of the bed in his boxer shorts, holding the phone in one hand and pounding his naked chest hard with the other.

Chloe had been lost in a dream in which she was making love with her boyfriend from college. The smell and the taste of it was exactly as it had been. Twenty-five years ago in a dorm room in a single bed. Joni Mitchell singing on the stereo.

And then the phone had rung.

The child had died after two days hooked up to machines, and a prayer vigil. They were donating the organs. No one blamed Jay. Her husband's fist left a bright red circle on his chest where he hit it. He hit it again.

"So what's your holiday look like?" the man ahead of her in line asks, looking at the beer and festive junk food in her cart.

Chloe's mouth opens, and she tries to form a word, but has no idea what the word would be. She swallows, still with her mouth open, and the man's face changes. It must look to him like she is about to cry. He says, "Are you all right?"

She shakes her head. She takes a step backward, pulling her cart with her as she goes, and the line behind her buckles, it seems, like some kind of human bridge—some grumbling, some sighing, an annoyed intake of breath. Perhaps they are envious, or pitying, or disdainful to see that Chloe is leaving the line for good, doing the unthinkable, absenting herself from the line she has been standing in for such a long time, finally even abandoning her cart, walking backward as she watches the man ahead of her recede with a concerned look on his face before he, too, steps out of the line and follows Chloe with his arms full of chips, which he dumps into her abandoned cart before taking her arm, guiding her out of the store and into the parking lot, to his car, leaving the cart and the line and the chips behind them for all of eternity.

The Skill

Impossible that Greta would be the first to learn this secret, this subtlety, this skill, whatever you wanted to call it. And to learn it so simply, so much like learning a first language. Like water pouring into a glass until it was almost full. That there weren't others who could also do this seemed so unlikely, but she'd never heard anyone speak of it, and never would. Not a word on the subject in the library. Not a single helpful Google hit.

It was so easy. All she'd had to do was stare at it—and even from a distance of twenty feet, and through the windshield of her stepmother's car, which separated herself from the suffering pigeon while her stepmother was in the grocery store, shopping for something for dinner.

("Want anything?" "No.")

All she'd done was watch it and whisper under her breath, precisely four times, *Please die, Please die, Please die, Please die.*

And all at once it had stopped its pitiful, heartbreaking hopping, its scrambling effort to get away from the parking lot that had killed it (some bitch in an SUV, who hadn't even slowed down) and to get back to something like nature. Grass. Tree. Nest. Wondering horribly what had happened to it, and what might happen next, while realizing that getting back would be impossible now. It would be like trying to go back in time. Before the affair. Before the divorce. Before her father remarried the mistress. Before they'd moved to this awful town so far from her real mother. To get back to the time when he'd called her mother his Morning Glory, and her his Baby Dumpling-Daisy.

That world was gone.

She had watched the whole thing happen. The pigeon in a swooping flight, heading for some scrap of bread near the wheel of a parked car, and the speeding SUV, and even with the windows rolled up Greta had heard the smack and witnessed the broken way the bird fell out of the air to the ground.

And then the struggle, the hopeless situation, the curb, too far away, and that SUV making a left turn out of the grocery store parking lot as if nothing had happened at all.

Greta's stepmother made a face when she came out of the store and saw the dead pigeon on the pavement, and veered her shopping cart far around it. She took a long time putting the paper bags in the trunk, and when she plopped back down into the driver's seat she said to Greta, wearily, "Is anything wrong?"

"No," Greta said, never mentioning the pigeon, which her step-mother also never mentioned, even when they passed within a few feet of it while driving out of the parking lot, and Greta looked out at it, hard:

A wad of pale purple feathers now. No blood. One beady eye—the only eye Greta could see—open. A damp, dark peace was in that, she thought, and thought of her father's face the day she rode a bicycle toward him without training wheels for the first time. . . . "You got it, girl!" he'd shouted. He was sweaty and red-faced and out of breath, as if he were the one who'd been peddling unsteadily down the side-walk toward himself, as if there were something like riding a bicycle in watching a child ride one.

On the pavement, looking up with that one eye, the pigeon seemed to be looking up at its own self flying away from itself.

"So, are we going to ride along in stony silence, Greta? Maybe I should turn the radio on?"

Greta shrugged a shoulder, and continued to stare out the window long after the pigeon was long gone.

The rest of Greta's childhood wound through a kind of thicket, and she emerged from it wearing a blindfold that someone had tied around her face that day in the grocery store parking lot. Some witch, some devil, some fairy godmother or guardian angel had tied it behind her head and whispered, *Don't take it off, whatever you do.*

And she never had, although she'd spent all those years knowing that she could.

It had tortured her and sustained her. This secret, supernatural power. This skill. She'd look at the side of her stepmother's face beside her in the car for a few terrifying seconds, and then look away, vowing never to look at the woman that closely, ever again, and she never did.

She did her homework and cleared the table after dinner. She took the garbage out on Fridays. She introduced her stepmother to her classmates and boyfriends at college, sent her cards on Mother's Day, thanked her for every meal she ever made, and held her in her arms on the day of her father's funeral as her stepmother sobbed and sobbed as if she were the little girl who had lost her father.

Greta watched her own children crawl into her stepmother's lap and call her Grandma. She helped the old woman fold her laundry. She drove her to the grocery store on Sundays.

And, all the time, Greta knew what she knew about the skill she had and would not use until finally one day there was a tube in her stepmother's throat. One eye was dead, and one was fixed on Greta—the parched lips opening and closing, the spotted skin, the limbs all turned into themselves like the branches of a terrible tree, and Greta kissed her stepmother's forehead then, took a step back, taking her in, before she said it four times under her breath, and then listened. Some radiant wind swirling around the dead woman. Some sound of grateful bliss.

"If a Stranger Approaches You about Carrying a Foreign Object with You onto the Plane"

Once there was a woman who was asked by a stranger to carry a foreign object with her onto a plane. When the stranger approached her, the woman was sitting at the edge of her chair a few feet from the gate out of which her plane was scheduled to leave. Her legs were crossed. She was wearing a black turtleneck and slim black pants. Black boots. Pearl studs in her ears. She was swinging the loose leg, the one that was tossed over the knee of the other— swinging it slowly and rhythmically, like a pendulum, as she tried to drink her latte in burning sips.

By the time the stranger approached her and asked her to carry the foreign object with her onto the plane, the woman had already owned that latte for at least twenty minutes, but it hadn't cooled a single degree. It was as if there were a thermonuclear process at work inside her cup—the steamed milk and espresso somehow generating together their own heat—and the tip of her tongue had been stung numb from trying to drink it, and the plastic nipple of the cup's white lid was smeared with her lipstick.

Her name was Kathy Bliss. She was anxious. At home, her two-year-old was sick, but she'd had to go to Maine anyway because she'd been asked to speak on behalf of the nonprofit for which she worked, and possibly thousands upon thousands of dollars would be

gifted to it by her hosts if she were able to conjure the right com-
bination of passion and desperation with which she was sometimes
able to speak on behalf of her nonprofit. She didn't much believe
in what they were doing, which was, to her mind, mostly justifying
the spending of their donations on computers and letterheads and
lunches with donors, but she had her eye on another nonprofit, one
devoted to curing a disease (or at least *publicizing* a disease) which
no one knew about until it was contracted, at which time the body
attacked itself, turning the skin into a suit of armor, petrifying the
internal organs one by one. The vice president of this nonprofit
had his eye on the regional directorship of the American Cancer
Society, she knew, and with some luck his position would be open,
and she would be ready to move into it.

Still, she'd always understood that you have to put your energy
into the place you are if you want to move on to another place;
and, on occasion, she could be convincing—something about the
podium, a bottle of water, a few notes, and all eyes on her—and there
was clearly no one else at her nonprofit who could even remotely
have been considered for this engagement. (Jen, with her multiple
piercings? Rob with his speech impediment?) She had to go.

The baby was sick, but the baby would be fine. Kathy Bliss had
a husband, after all, who would take care of their baby. He was the
baby's father, for God's sake. This wasn't 1952. The man had a Ph.D.
in compassion. Who was she to think the baby would be any better
off with her there just because she was *of a certain gender*? And if she
hadn't had to go to Maine, Garrett would have gone to work himself, which would have left only one parent at home anyway, doing
the same thing either way—cuddling, cleaning up puke, taking the
temp, filling the sippy cup with cold water.

Still, Kathy Bliss felt a pain, which she knew, intellectually, was
imaginary, but nonetheless was excruciating, hovering around a few
inches above her breasts, as if only moments ago something adhe-
sive—a bandage, duct tape, a baby—had been ripped away from her
bare flesh and taken a top layer of cellular material with it.

The latte had scalded her tongue (just the tip) to the point that she could feel, when she moved it across the ridge behind teeth, the rough little bumps of it gone completely dead—just a prickling dullness. Without the taste buds to interfere, Kathy Bliss could really feel the ridge behind the back of her teeth, the place where the bone smoothed into flesh, the difference between what was there for now and what, when she was dead, would be left. She took another sip. Better. Maybe it had cooled down a bit, or maybe her tongue couldn't register the heat of it anymore. That was probably dangerous, she thought. The way people got scalded. Their nerve endings dulled, and they stepped into the tub without knowing it would cook them.

"Sorry," the stranger said after his pant leg brushed her knee, but she didn't really look at him, not yet. His tan belt was at eye level, nothing remarkable about it, and then he was gone.

As was always the case in airports, there was a small crowd of confused people (the elderly, the poor, some foreigners) standing patiently in a line they didn't need to stand in, and a woman behind a counter who was waving them away one by one as they approached her with their fully sufficient pieces of paper.

"We'll be boarding in forty minutes," the woman said over and over, refusing to smile, make eye contact, or answer questions. The woman had a spectacular hairpiece on top of her head. A kind of beehive with fronds. When she waved, the fronds shivered, caught the light, looking fountainlike, or like incandescent antennas. Although the woman had dark skin (tanning booth?), her real hair was a pale pink-blond beneath the hairpiece, which was the synthetic blond of a Barbie doll. What had the woman been thinking, Kathy Bliss wondered, that morning at the mirror, placing it atop her head. What had she believed she would look like with that thing on her head? Had she *wanted* to look the way she did— shocking, alien, a creature out of an illustrated Hans Christian Andersen?

Many years before, when Kathy Bliss was a college student, in an incident that had, she believed, changed and defined her forever, she'd come across a dead body in the Arboretum. A woman.

Stabbed. Mostly bones and some scraps of clothing—and she (Kathy Bliss, not the dead woman) had run screaming.

It had been a very quick glimpse, so of course she hadn't known at the time that the body was that of a woman, or that the woman had been stabbed, knew nothing of the details until she was given them later by the police. Still, she knew that she must have stood there open-mouthed for at least a second or two (she had been running on a trail but gone off of it to pee) because she clearly saw, or *remembered* seeing, that there were bees in that dead woman's hair.

When a few people left the line, a few more entered it. All over the airport, there were such sad, small crowds. They hesitated together at every counter, not ready to believe that all was well, not able to so easily accept the assurance that they already had what they needed, that they had found their proper places so quickly and had only now to wait. Kathy Bliss herself had forced one such crowd to part for her when she entered the terminal, pulling her suitcase on wheels behind her as she made her way to security. She could feel their eyes on her back as she passed, knew they were probably loathing and admiring in equal measure her swift professional purposefulness. *She* knew where she was going. *She'd* done this a million times.

But, to her ears anyway, the wheels of her luggage made the sound of a spit turning quickly (but with some effort) over a burning pit, as she dragged it behind her. She had no idea why. They weren't rusty. It was a fairly new bag. It had never been left out in the rain or pulled through the mud. But there it was, the sound of a spit, turning. A pig on that spit. An apple in its mouth. That final humiliation. *We shall eat you, Pig.*

She couldn't believe it when, at the *SAVe a LIFe!* picnic that summer, that they'd actually *done* that, actually roasted a pig on a spit with an apple crammed into its mouth.

At first, she hadn't noticed it because she'd been busy meeting and greeting. ("Yes, yes, of course I remember. Nice to see you again. Thank you for coming.")

But after she'd filled her glass with punch and had just tipped the glass to her lips, she'd seen it out of the corner of her eye, taken one step toward it, seen it fully then, and reeled—literally reeled—and splashed pink punch onto her chest, where it trickled down in a sweet zigzagging rivulet between her breasts.

Luckily, she'd been wearing a low-cut dress, also pink.

"Whoa," the college president she'd been standing next to said when she reeled. "Friend of yours or something? Are you a vegetarian?"

"Jesus," she'd said, "I am now," turning her back to the spit, trying to smile. But there was a cool film of sweat all over her body, as if each pore had opened in a moment, coating her with dew. "What a spectacle."

"Isn't that the point?" the college president had said.

"Because of heightened security measures," the ceiling droned, *"we ask that you report any unattended luggage. If a stranger should approach you and ask you to carry a foreign object with you onto a plane, please contact a member of security personnel immediately. . . ."*

"Excuse me?" the stranger said, taking a seat beside her.

Kathy Bliss turned, swinging her leg off her knee, placing both black boots beside one another on the floor.

"Yes?"

The stranger was young and handsome. He had dark hair and tan skin and large brown eyes. Slender fingers. What appeared to be an actual gold Rolex on his wrist. He was wearing a white shirt with a red tie and a black leather jacket. An Arab, she thought right away, and then felt bad for thinking it. He had no accent. She could tell that already from the two words he'd spoken. He was an American, not an "Arab." He was probably more American than she was, her mother's parents having stumbled into this country from Liverpool, broke, in the twenties, her paternal grandparents having dashed across the Canadian border in the thirties in search of higher-paying employment with the U.S. Postal Service.

Still, it must be awful, she thought, to *look* like an Arab in an airport these days. It must have felt, she supposed, like wearing a scarlet A. Everyone staring, either wondering suspiciously about you and feeling guilty about wondering, or feeling suspicious and self-righteous about staring and wondering. "I'm sorry to bother you," the stranger said. "Are you, by any chance, going to Portland?"

"Yes," Kathy Bliss said.

"Well—" he smiled, and then his breast pocket began to play the theme from the *Lone Ranger* loudly and digitally, and he reached into it and fumbled around for a moment until it stopped and he said, "Sorry," shaking his head. For a crazy second Kathy Bliss thought of asking him to check the caller ID, to make sure her husband wasn't trying to reach her with some news about the baby (she'd turned her own cell off to conserve the battery, and would check it just before she got on the plane)—but, of course, this stranger had nothing to do with her baby.

"Can I help you?" she asked.

The man had a tiny gold cross in his left earlobe. It was really very beautiful—and strange, too, how masculine that little earring made him look with the dark shadow of beard on his chiseled jaw-line, and how masculine he made that earring by wearing it in his ear, with its foiled brilliance. A small, bold statement. It might have been a religious statement or a fashion statement, what difference did it make?

"Yes, but please," he said, "if this sounds strange to you, just send me away."

"Okay?" she said. A question.

"Okay," he said. "I'm supposed to be going to Portland for my mother's seventieth birthday, but I just got a call from my girl-friend telling me—" he smiled ruefully, rolled his eyes to the ceiling, "—I'm sorry, I should make something up here, but I'll just tell you the truth. She's pregnant. And she's flipping out. And I feel like," he tossed some emptiness into the air with his palms, making a ges-ture she'd seen men make many times in response to women's emo-tional states, "honestly—I think I ought to go buy her an engage-ment ring *today*, and get my butt over to her apartment. I mean, this isn't a disaster. Or it doesn't *have* to be. We were getting mar-ried anyway, and we knew we might get pregnant. We weren't even using any—" He shook his head. "I'm sorry, *really* sorry, to be filling you in on all these details. I'd made it through security, I was planning to just go and come back maybe even tonight, and then I realized—I just realized I shouldn't go at all. That I should go straight back to my girlfriend right now." He inhaled, looked at Kathy Bliss as if trying to gauge her reaction. "I'm sorry," he said, "to fill you, a complete stranger, in on these sordid details."

Kathy Bliss tried to laugh sympathetically. She shook her head a little. Shrugged. "It's okay," she said. "Been there, done that!"

The stranger laughed pretty hard at this. His teeth were very straight and white, although one of the front ones had what looked to be a hairline crack in it. A very thin gray crack. Her two-year-old, Connor, had just recently gotten so many new teeth that it surprised her every time he opened his mouth. The teeth were like little dabs of meringue. Clean and white and peaked. She liked to smell his breath. It was as if there were a pure little spring in there. His mouth smelled like mineral water.

"Well, there you have it," the stranger said. "I guess, if nothing else, we're all here because *somebody'd* been there and done that."

"That, too," Kathy Bliss said. "But, I mean, I have a child. It's a great thing."

"Yeah," he said. "I'm starting to forget, in all this hysteria, the great fact that I'm going to be a dad—"

"Well, congratulations from me," Kathy Bliss said. She felt the warm implication of tears starting somewhere around her sinuses, and swallowed. She changed her latte cup from her right hand to her left, reached over the metal armrest, and offered it to him. He shook it, smiling. Then he shook his own hand as if it had been burned. "Jeez," he said, "that's one burning handshake."

"My latte," she said. "It's like molten lava."

"I guess so," he said.

The stranger was wearing khaki pants with very precisely ironed creases. For a quick second Kathy Bliss wondered if his girlfriend was also an Arab, and then she remembered that she had no way of knowing that *he* was an Arab, and far more evidence, anyway, that he *wasn't*—and reminded herself that it didn't matter anyway. So, maybe his parents had been born in Egypt, or Iraq. The color of his skin was beautiful. A warm milky brown. She felt a pang of jealousy about the girlfriend, lying on their bed at home, not knowing that this beautiful stranger was making desperate plans to buy her a diamond that day. What a thing, this life. Love. God, when it worked, it really worked! She had, herself, fallen in love with her husband upon first sight. She'd been given his name as the best shrink in town for the kind of problem she was having—which was spending every minute of her day trying not to think about the dead body in the Arboretum for two solid years after she'd seen it—and she had no sooner settled herself in the chair across from his, and he'd crossed his legs, looking more anxious and frightened than she, herself, the *patient*, felt, that she knew she wanted to marry him. And he'd cured her, too. Without drugs. A few behavior modifications. A rubber band around her wrist, a mantra, a series of self-punishments and rewards.

"Well, to make a long story short," the stranger said, "my girlfriend's freaking out back at our apartment, and my mother's turning seventy in Portland, and I'm her only son, who's such a scoundrel and an ingrate, not to mention morally reprehensible for impregnating someone he's not married to, *yet*, that he's not even showing up for her party, so—" and here he shook his head and looked directly into Kathy Bliss's eyes, "I wonder if I, a stranger, could ask you, a passenger, to carry a foreign object with you onto the plane?"

"Oh my God," Kathy Bliss said. "All these years I was wondering if anyone was ever going to ask me that."

"I think," the stranger said, "now is the point at which you ought to contact security personnel—like, right away."

"Yes," she said, "I think I may have heard an announcement pertaining to that. And I've always wondered to myself what kind of idiot would actually do such a thing, like carry a foreign object onto a plane."

"Well," the stranger said, "here's the object you've been waiting your whole life to carry with you onto the plane."

Out of a pocket in the inner lining of his coat, the stranger produced a narrow rectangular box wrapped in gold paper. He sighed. "It's a gold necklace, and if you'd be so foolhardy as to carry it with you onto the plane, I'd call my brother and have him meet you at baggage claim and get it to the party this evening. *But,*" he waved his slender fingers around over the box, "I totally understand if you think that's nuts."

"I have no problem with it," she said. "Don't worry, I won't contact security personnel."

"Let me open it for you, at least," he said, "so you know you're not carrying a bomb—"

"If you managed to get a bomb in that little package," she said, "you deserve to have it carried by a passenger onto the plane."

She regretted the joke even as she said it, saw the towers dissolving into dust on her television again. It had been on the floor because the entertainment center had not yet arrived (it was being custom-built somewhere in Illinois) and there was no table or counter big enough to put the television on. The baby was crying (eight weeks old), so she'd had to stand and pace with his hot little face leaking tears onto her shoulders as those towers collapsed at her feet. The front door had been open, and it had smelled to her as if the stone-blue perfect sky out there were dissolving in talcumish particles of dried flowers—such a beautiful day it horrified her. An illusion dipped in blue. She could have walked with her baby straight out the front door or right into the big-screen TV of it, and they might have turned, themselves, into nothing but subatomic particles, blue light, perfume.

There was nothing funny about terrorism. Nothing even remotely funny about terrorism. Still, she was from the Midwest, and it seemed like a long time ago already. No more National Guard in the airport—those boys with their big weapons trying not to look bored and out of place around every corner. She had, herself, only been to New York a few times, and never to those towers, having only glimpsed them from her plane as it banked into LaGuardia. From the plane, they'd looked like Legos, and no matter how real she knew it all was, on the television, on the floor, it had not looked real. And the least likely plane a terrorist would want to blow up or hijack was one traveling from Grand Rapids, Michigan, to Portland, Maine. Right? "Don't unwrap that," she said. "It's exquisite. I trust you."

"I insist," he said. "This is too weird and too much of a . . . cliché. I have my dignity!" He laughed. "And in any case, I will doubt your sanity if you don't let me open it. I can't have a crazy woman delivering my mother's birthday present—"

"No," Kathy Bliss said, snatching the little present off his lap. "You'll never get it wrapped like this again. It's like a little dream. I'd be insane if I thought you could get anything *but* a necklace in that box."

He made his mouth into a zero, and sighed, loosened his tie a little by inserting his index finger between the knot and his collar. From somewhere on the other side of the wall of screens that listed arrivals and departures, a baby began to cry, and the feeling came back to her—the ripping, intensely, as if yet another layer of skin, or whatever was underneath her skin, were being pulled off her torso in one quick yank. The stranger took the cell phone out of his pocket and said, "I'll call my brother. Can I tell him your name. I'll have him at baggage claim—I mean," he interrupted himself here, "I'm assuming that's where you'll be going—" he looked at the black bag at her feet—"Did you check luggage?"

"Yes," she said. "I mean, no. But I can go to baggage claim, no problem. Tell him—"

"I'll have him carry a sign, with your name on it, okay?"

"Yes. Kathy Bliss."

"Bliss?" He smiled. "Like, 'bliss'?"

"Yes," she said. "Like the Joseph Campbell thing. 'Follow your bliss.'"

He smiled, but she could tell he hadn't heard of Joseph Campbell, or the advice of Joseph Campbell. She had, herself, been in graduate school when the PBS series with Bill Moyers had aired, and gotten together every Tuesday night with a group of women from her Mind, Brain, and Violence Seminar to watch it. A lot of joking about Bliss, and following it, had been made. When she'd get up to go to the bathroom or to get a beer out of the refrigerator, someone always pretended to follow her.

"*We would like to begin boarding passengers on Flight 5236 to Portland, Maine. Passengers traveling with small children or needing special assistance . . .*"

"That's me," she said.

"Yes," he said. "Of course. I'll make the call after you board. But let me tell you, my brother—he's twenty-two, but he looks a lot like me. I haven't seen him in a year, and sometimes he has long hair and sometimes he shaves his head, so," he shrugged, "who knows. But he's about 5'9", 160 pounds—"

Kathy Bliss slipped the gold-wrapped box into her black bag carefully, so he could see that he could trust her with it. "Well," she said, "he'll have my name on a piece of paper, right. It'll be simple."

"Am I right, the plane's supposed to land at 12:51?" the stranger asked, peeking into the inner lining of his suit coat again, as if to look at his own unnecessary itinerary.

"Yep," she said. "12:51, assuming we're on time."

"Here," he said, hurrying with a piece of paper and a pen he'd taken from the pocket of his suitcoat, "my brother's name is Mack Kaloustian. He'll be there. Or I'll kill him, and he knows it."

Kaloustian. Armenian. Kathy Bliss blinked and saw a spray of bullets raking through a family in a stand of trees on a mountain top, a mother shielding her child, collapsing onto him. That child might have been this stranger's grandmother. And then they were boarding her row—12. Kathy Bliss stood up and extended her hand to the stranger. "Good luck to you," she said with all the warmth she could generate with only four words. The second word, *luck,* caught in her throat—a little emotional fishhook made out of consonants—because it was all so lovely, and simple, and lucky. Nothing but goodness in it for anyone. And her part in this sweet small drama moved her deeply, too—this gesture she was making of pure human camaraderie, this nonprofit venture, this small recognition of the cliché *we're all in this together*. That it mattered. Love. Family. The stranger. The favor. The bond of trust between them. He knew she wouldn't disappear into Portland with his gold necklace. She knew he wouldn't—what? Send her onto a plane with an explosive? He shook her hand so warmly it was like a hug. He said, "I can't tell you how much I appreciate this," and she said, "Of course. I'm happy to be able to help," and then she walked backward so she could extend the moment of their smiling and parting, and then turned, inhaling, and began the dull and claustrophobic process of boarding her plane.

Kathy Bliss had been born and raised in a little stone house at the edge of a deep forest. "Honest to God," she always had to say after giving someone this piece of information about herself for the first time. "But it was nothing like you're imagining."

Her father had worked for a minimum security prison, and the prison had been the thing her bedroom window faced, its high cyclone fencing topped by hundreds of yards of coiled razor wire. In the summer, the sun rising in the east over the prison turned that wire into a blinding fretwork, all spun-sugar and baroque glitter, as if the air had been embroidered with silver thread by a gifted witch. She'd squint at it pretending that what her bedroom faced was an enchanted castle, as if the little stone house at the edge of the dark forest really were something from a fairy tale. But it was a sedentary childhood. Her parents wouldn't let her play in the yard or wait outside for the bus because, if there were an escape, she would make too good a hostage, being the prison director's daughter. For this reason, Kathy Bliss rarely had the chance to see the prisoners milling around behind that razor wire, wearing their orange jumpsuits, and was able, therefore, to imagine them handsome and gallant as knights.

She and her mother had moved, when Kathy was nine, after her father died from an illness that announced itself first as bleeding gums, and then paralysis, and then he was just gone. She was thinking about this blip in her first years—the stone house, the barbed-wire castle—and watching the other passengers struggle onto the plane, shoving their heavy luggage into overhead compartments, the fat ones sweating, the thin ones trembling, the mothers with babies and little children looking blissfully burdened, when a voice came over the plane's intercom and said, "If there is a Katherine Bliss on board, could she please press the flight attendant call button now?"

"Oh my God," Kathy Bliss said so loudly that an old woman standing in the aisle next to her whirled around and hit the call button for her. "Is that you?" the old woman said, as if she knew what they were calling Kathy Bliss about, as if everyone knew. "Yes," she said. "I forgot to check my messages." "Oh dear," the old woman said. The skin hung off her face in gray rags, and yet she'd made herself up carefully that morning, with tastefully understated foundation and blush, the kind of replica of life that would cause all gathered around her casket to say, "She just looks as if she's sleeping." There began a cold trickling at the tip of Kathy Bliss's spine, and then it turned into a fine mist coating every inch of her. She could not close her mouth. She tried to stand, but there were so many people in the aisle she couldn't get out of her seat, although the old woman had turned to face the strangers surging forward and put a bony arm in front of her as if to try to block their passage. "Ma'am," a flight attendant said from ten feet behind that line, looking at the old woman. "Are you Mrs. Bliss?"

"No," the old woman said, and pointed to Kathy. "This is Mrs. Bliss."

"We have a message for you, Mrs. Bliss," the flight attendant called over the shoulders of the passengers in the aisle. She was a huge blond beauty, a Norse goddess. Someone who might stand on a mountain peak with a bolt of lightning in her fist. The crowd in the aisle dissolved to make way for her, and she pressed a folded piece of paper into Kathy Bliss's shaking hand. *Baby in hospital. Call home now. Husband.*

It was a week later—after the long pale nights at his cribside in the hospital, taking turns pretending to sleep as the other paced, the tests, and the antibiotics, and the failure of the first ones to fight off the infection, and the terrifying night when the baby didn't wake during his injection, and they could clearly see the residency doctor's hand shaking as he punched the emergency button. It was after they'd begun a whole new life on the children's floor. Sesame Street in the lounge all day, as if the world were being run by benevolent toys, and then CNN scrolling its silent, redundant messages to them all night below images of the cynical and maimed. After they'd gotten to know the nurses. It was after Kathy Bliss had fallen in love, madly, with one doctor after another—not a sexual love, but a deep wild worship of the archetype, a reverent adulation of the Healer— and then grown to despise them one by one, and then to see them merely as human beings. It was after she'd spent some self-conscious moments on her knees in the hospital chapel, which turned into deep semiconscious communions with the Almighty as the hospital intercom called out its mundane codes and locations in the hallway behind her—and the baby was taking fluids, and then solids, and then given a signature of release, and the nurses hugged Kathy Bliss and her husband, and let their hands wave magically, baptismally, over the head of the baby, who laughed, sputtered, still a little weak, scarlet-cheeked, but very much of this world, and cured for the next leg of the journey into the future, when they packed up the stuffed animals and picture books and headed for home—it was after all these events had come to an end that Kathy Bliss remembered the foreign object, given to her by the stranger, which had stayed where she'd tucked it into her carry-on luggage, where she'd left it in the hallway of her house, tossed under a table, in a panic, on her brief stop there between the airport and the hospital.

Garrett had gone to work, and the baby was napping in a patch of sunlight that poured green and gold through the front door onto the living room floor. It was a warm late summer day. The phone had been unplugged the night before, and stayed that way. She hadn't turned the television on once since they'd come home. The silence swelled and receded in a manner that would have been imperceivable to her only two weeks before, but which now seemed sacred, full of implication, a kind of immaculate tableau rolled out over the neighborhood in the middle of the day when no one was anywhere, and only the cats crossed the streets, padding in considerate quiet on their starry little paws. She glanced at the black bag.

She got down on her knees and pulled the bag to her, and removed the umbrella, and the pink makeup bag, and the folded black sweater, the brother's name, *Mack Kaloustian* (but hadn't the stranger said he was his mother's only son?), and saw it there, the box, in its gold paper, and recognized it only vaguely, as neither a gift nor a recrimination, a threat or a blessing.

She didn't open it, but imagined herself opening it. Imagined herself as a passenger on that plane, unable to resist it. Holding it to her ear. Shaking it, maybe. Lifting the edge of the gold paper, tearing it away from the box. And then, the certain, brilliant cataclysm that would follow. The lurching of unsteady weight in the sky, and then the inertia, followed by tumbling. The numbing sensation of great speed and realization in your face. She'd been a fool to take it with her onto the plane. It could have killed them all.

Or, the simple gold braid of it.

Tasteful. Elegant. A thoughtful gift chosen by a devoted son for his beloved mother. And she imagined taking the necklace out of the box, holding it up to her own neck at the mirror, admiring the glint of it around her neck—this bit of love and brevity snatched from the throat of a stranger—wearing it with an evening gown, passing it down as an heirloom to her children.

Who was to say, she thought to herself as she began to peel the gold paper away, that something stolen, without malice or intent, is any less yours than something you've been given?

Acknowledgments

Some of these stories have been previously published in *Ploughshares* ("If a Stranger Approaches You about Carrying a Foreign Object with You onto the Plane"), *Epoch* ("Mona," "Our Father"), *The Michigan Quarterly Review* ("Joyride"), *The Florida Review* ("The Barge"), *Fantasy & Science Fiction Magazine* ("Search Continues for Elderly Man"). "Melody," was first published by *Five Chapters* under the title "The Amicable Divorce." "If a Stranger Approaches You about Carrying a Foreign Object with You onto the Plane" was reprinted in *The Pushcart Anthology*. It also received the Cohen Award for Fiction from *Ploughshares*, 2007. "The Barge" was reprinted in The Pushcart Anthology, 2013. "Search Continues for Elderly Man" was reprinted in *Real Unreal: Best American Fantasy 3*.

LAURA KASISCHKE

has published eight collections of poetry and eight novels. This is her first story collection. She has been the recipient of a Guggenheim Fellowship, two grants from the National Endowment for the Arts, several Pushcart Prizes, and the 2011 National Book Critics Circle Award in Poetry for *Space in Chains*. She lives in Chelsea, Michigan, with her husband and son, and teaches in the MFA program at the University of Michigan.